COSMIC CATS &
FANTASTIC FURBALLS

COSMIC CATS &
FANTASTIC FURBALLS

FANTASY AND SCIENCE FICTION STORIES
WITH CATS

MARY A. TURZILLO

WFP
WordFire Press

EBook ISBN: 978-1-68057-280-3
Trade Paperback ISBN: 978-1-68057-279-7
Dust Jacket Hardcover ISBN: 978-1-68057-281-0
Case Bind Hardcover ISBN: 978-1-68057-282-7

Cover design by Janet McDonald
Cover artwork images by Adobe Stock
Kevin J. Anderson, Art Director
Published by
WordFire Press, LLC
PO Box 1840
Monument CO 80132
Kevin J. Anderson & Rebecca Moesta, Publishers
WordFire Press eBook Edition 2022
WordFire Press Trade Paperback Edition 2022
WordFire Press Hardcover Edition 2022
Printed in the USA
Join our WordFire Press Readers Group for
sneak previews, updates, new projects, and giveaways.
Sign up at wordfirepress.com

CONTENTS

DEDICATION

To Jane Ann and the guys at Missing Buffalo Farm:
John-Paul, Jenn, Jordan, Roxie, J.D., Nathan,
and Nicholas.

STEAK TARTARE AND THE CATS OF GARI BABAKIN STATION

EARTHLINGS WERE COMING to attack the cats this very afternoon. And where was Benoît?

Had she really considered licking his earlobe while he was reporting on the new cheese flavonoids? As if he were a surly tomcat, like this handsome furball now rubbing her legs?

Ah, Lucile, she thought, *so impulsive we are! The boy's not all that sexy; he never combs his hair or gets it cut, or even washes it often.*

He had a certain something, though. Think how he lashed out at the Earth inspectors who came through a year ago trying to murder the feral cats in tunnel M. The inspectors wanted to vent that corridor and let the cats die of decompression. Benoît put them in their place.

Those Earth people! They need cats. Cats to sleep with, to feed, to pet, to tease with bits of string, to get a little rough with and wind up with a bitten finger or a scratched cheek. That would rearrange their psychic furniture.

Benoît used to say, "They have cats on Earth, too, so what the hell's their problem?"

But not cats like those of Gari Babakin Station.

Where *was* Benoît? As Supervisor of Flavor Engineering and

the mayor's third in command, he was supposed to greet them so she could make a late, more impressive entrance.

A message came in that a rocketplane had arrived from Borealopolis carrying Terran supervisors.

Providentially, Benoît slunk in just then, running fingers through his greasy hair. He had been trying to grow a beard, and looked endearingly like an adolescent ferret.

"They're here," Lucile said levelly. "And me in this nasty old jumpsuit! At least I put on perfume this morning." She swung around to Benoît. "You were supposed to greet them."

"I didn't think they'd follow through on their threat," Benoît said. He picked up the cat that had been pestering Lucile and scratched between its ears. At least she thought it was the same cat. All the cats looked the same, small polydactyl tabbies in varying shades of dark gray, with pink noses, all descended from the same pregnant queen that somebody smuggled into Gari Babakin Station twenty Mars years before.

"It's about the cats."

"Oh, yeah. That. They said some dumb thing about a parasite or virus. I thought they were talking about crabs."

"Benoît!" she hissed. "They are not sending a delegation from Earth or even from Borealopolis to stop an epidemic of crab lice." She clawed through her desk drawer for her makeup kit, but found only a purple lace garter belt she had misplaced.

"So? Why do they always have to pick on us?"

Benoît exasperated her. He got more adolescent every day. He had a PhD in xenonutrition, for heaven's sake!

No, it wouldn't be worth seducing him, even if he was one of the few non-disgusting men on the station she hadn't bedded. "Listen, Benoît, they're coming through the front airlock. Could you entertain them? I have to go back to my apartment and change." What was in her closet? The red frock with the keyhole above the derriere. Perfect.

When she got back, nicely turned out in the black faux tux since the red frock had a bigarade sauce stain near the plunge of the neckline, she found Benoît and three strangers in the reception room off the main airlock. Benoît's hands were jammed in his pockets, his eyes narrowed with paranoid hostility. The three strangers—two dowdy-looking women and a slender youngish man with chopped-off hair and depilatory burns on his cheeks—were still in environment suits, shrinking away from the clowder of cats weaving in and around their legs.

The man pulled off his glove, strode forward to shake hands with Lucile, faltered as if he had changed his mind about touching her, then finally seemed to conquer his squeamishness and held his hand out like a Ping-Pong paddle. "I'm Godfrey Worcester," he said. "You're the head of the station? Martialle Lafayette?" He used the feminine of the Martian formal title for citizen.

Lucile took his hand and held it in both of hers. "No, no, Jean-Marie took a personal day. I'm in charge in his absence." What a shame Jean-Marie liked his wine so much, especially before lunch.

"Jean-Marie? A man? We really need to talk to Martial Lafayette." He switched to the masculine form. "You would be?"

"I would be Lucile Raoul. I'll send for Jean-Marie." She gazed into Godfrey's hazel eyes. He was a handsome, trim fellow despite the fact that his barber apparently hated him. She liked these naive types.

She turned to the two women. "May I take your suits? Your suitliners? We have some chic little dusters you can change into while you're in the station." She tried not to roll her eyes. Both women apparently had been victimized by the same barber as Godfrey, and she shuddered to think what they wore under their suitliners. Neither of them seemed to have the imagination to go naked underneath, although you never could tell.

Benoît sprang to attention. "I know what you're after, and we will resist to the death."

Lucile let go of Godfrey's hand and went to Benoît. "Benoît, dear, let these nice people have their say. But first, may I offer coffee and a pastry?"

"Where do you get real coffee?" asked the frumpier of the two women suspiciously.

"But my dear, we didn't get it. We manufacture it. Alain, our head molecular gastronomist, is just a genius with esters."

"He's the one that concocted the wine you sent us?" the tall woman asked. She was wriggling out of her suit, revealing a suitliner in a ghastly shade of pink that she apparently thought she could pass off as station day-wear. Lucile tried not to look.

"No, no, we have a special vigneron. But—"

Benoît interrupted. "We won't reveal his name. Your goons will kidnap him and lock him up in some forced labor laboratory."

Lucile looked daggers at Benoît. His eyes flashed, but he shut up.

Lucile escorted the trio (their clumsy gait in Mars gravity betrayed their recent arrival from Earth) to a patisserie on the upper level. The proprietor had coaxed a container of violets into bloom in the center of the room, under the mirror-maze skylight. The air smelled of cinnamon, coffee, and butter.

"Where's this Jean-Marie Lafayette?" the taller woman asked. Dr. Kermilda Wrothe was her name, Lucile had managed to find out. The shorter woman, who resembled a starved gerbil, was Dr. Hilda Wriothesley. "We can't be wasting time. This is a matter of public health."

Just then, two of the station cats—both wore purple bows around their necks, so Lucile concluded they belonged to the proprietor—started fighting, snarling, hissing, shrieking. The larger cat was apparently trying to mount the smaller, or maybe it was the other way around.

"I sent a message to his apartment. He'll be here as soon as he wakes up. Monsieur, may we have coffee all round, and a tray of your pastries?"

The coffee and pastries arrived and the three strangers eyed them with suspicion and desire.

Benoît said, "You can just forget it. You can't make us kill the cats. They are our soul."

Godfrey sat up straighter and said, "Oh, come now. Not only are you overrun with cats, but you are all infected with *Toxoplasma gondii*, and it's destroying your personalities as well as probably causing birth defects."

Benoît jumped up and leaned over the table, nose to nose with Godfrey. "That's slander, punk. First of all, impugning our personalities is tantamount to admitting that you want to enslave everybody on this station, take our proprietary secrets for wine and cheese making, and then wipe us out. Second, no child has been born on this station for over fifteen Mars years."

It was the longest speech Benoît had made in the entire time Lucile had known him. She stirred her coffee and sipped daintily. Under the table, she drove her spike heel into Benoît's instep.

He turned to her, bewildered.

"What Benoît is saying," she purred, "is that we are well aware of the issues involved in *Toxoplasma gondii* infection, but we feel that you are, shall we say, trying to impose your cultural values on us. I mean, as non-toxoplasmotic people."

Hilda spoke up for the first time. "Surely you can't mean that you enjoy the cultural values, as you call them, of being infected by a parasite?"

"That's exactly what she means, you constipated hag!" Benoît half rose and yelled in her face.

Lucile kicked him again, harder, and he sat down, deflated. She continued, "We prefer to think of *Toxoplasma gondii* as a kind of beneficial symbiont."

"That is just outrageous!" said Dr. Hilda Wriothesley. "We've monitored your communications. Analysis shows that your men are paranoid, poorly organized, and brain-damaged, while your women are—well, they're—"

"Stylish and attractive to the opposite sex?" Lucile purred. Her gaze traveled over the gaudy, shapeless coveralls the two women wore.

Godfrey stared at her, openmouthed.

She flicked a smile at him, as if they shared a delicious secret.

Godfrey cleared his throat, then started up a presentation from his finger computer, flashing the slides on the tabletop. "Top scientists at Utopia University have developed a virus which kills *Toxoplasma gondii* while leaving the host unharmed. It works very well with humans, and while there have been minor side effects in feline subjects, we feel that it is a viable solution to a public health problem that could otherwise spread beyond Gari Babakin Station and infect all of Mars."

She let him drone on. She'd heard it all before, but she enjoyed watching his lips. She'd love to get better acquainted with him, but there might not be time before he had to return to Borealopolis. And then there was the problem of Hilda and Kermilda. Entrusting them to the tender mercies of Benoît was out of the question, but maybe when Jean-Marie woke up, he could take them on a tour of the greenhouse vineyards.

When Godfrey turned off the presentation, she put her hand lightly on his wrist. "Dr. Worcester—Godfrey—you do make a point, but we really like our lifestyle here. We could put this to a referendum—but would we force the cure on people who didn't want it?" She had revolting images of herself dressed as badly as these two victims of the cult of sensible shoes.

"You're willing to forgo the joys of parenthood, then? True, you've enforced strict birth control via the air supply, but surely your women must yearn at times for motherhood."

She sighed. Now he was playing to her weak side. A charming little baby girl, to dress in pretty little frocks, to feed greenhouse strawberries and tidbits of pastry, to teach charming songs, to love, love, love—but *Toxoplasma gondii* could cause great harm to fetuses: blindness and encephalitis.

However, on the bright side, she was already seropositive with the parasite, so she reasoned that her future offspring was safe. She was sure. Almost. She need only protect the child from infection until its immune system was fully developed. She could surely arrange that.

However, she hadn't yet met anyone she trusted to father her adorable child. She smiled lingeringly at Godfrey, and he flushed slightly.

Benoît's eyes flicked warily from her to Godfrey. "You part of that Mars-needs-more-babies movement?"

Godfrey's lips turned white and pinched. "No, no! We just feel—well, your station's culture has—problems conforming to the overall community values of Martian life."

"And our culture deviates how?"

Hilda threw up her hands. "People sleeping until midday! Bed-hopping! Nobody cares whether the filing and maintenance are done properly, or at all! Not meeting planet-wide quotas! You put it kindly by saying the parasite makes women more gregarious, albeit at the expense of domestic tranquility, but the men, the men here—"

"Are more original," Lucile said.

"They have intellectual deficits!" Kermilda barked.

"They think outside the box. They aren't intimidated by common so-called wisdom," Lucile continued smoothly.

"Like cats," said Benoît.

And, in fact, the two squabbling cats were now a picture of cuddly affection, purple ribbons and all, under a table grooming each other. Lucile suppressed a smile, imagining Hilda and Kermilda doing the same. Except of course they would be repulsed by saliva.

She returned her gaze to them. "Gari Babakin Station excels in contributing innovative ideas to the greater Martian civilization."

Godfrey made a show of turning off his data ring. "Well, none of this means anything at all, because NutriTopia Ares, which I must remind you owns every molecule in this station, has authorized me to release the virus as soon as feasible."

He and the two women drained the last drops of their coffee, got up, and left.

After a stunned moment, Benoît leaned over. "Did they already release the virus, without talking to Jean-Marie?"

Lucile glanced at his worried face. "That's not the question you should be asking, Benoît. The issue is, what will the virus do?"

"Turn us into impotent zombies."

She sighed. "I don't know if the personality effects can be reversed once the *Toxoplasma gondii* takes root. The question is whether their virus will kill the cats. Or," she added, "us."

Lucile was not as worried as she sounded. In fact, she wasn't even sure the scientists of NutriTopia Ares had a technology to destroy *Toxoplasma gondii* oocysts. Previous attempts, with sulfadiazine and pyrimethamine-type drugs, had been unsuccessful, although they had certainly made enough people nauseated and anemic. Still—

Everybody at Gari Babakin Station knew their universal toxoplasmosis infection came from an infected pregnant cat named Muguet. They even accepted the evidence that it might raise women's intelligence and lower men's.

There had been a problem with the water filtration system early on in the history of the station, and unfortunately it kept getting recontaminated by oocysts shed either by cats or by humans. The citizens had stopped trying to fight it.

Lucile had arrived at the station at the age of eight, and stayed when her parents left to go back to Earth when she was twenty-three. She had no idea what she'd be like if she'd never ingested the oocysts, but she did, if she were honest, think herself more attractive and better dressed than the average Martialle.

As to Benoît, when he had arrived at the station three years ago, he had been meticulous in his habits. He kept tidy notebooks of his experiments in food engineering and wore his hair and mustache short and neat. He had planned to stay only a Martian summer, but somehow he'd abandoned his original plans. His neatness quotient had gone all to hell after four months; Lucile remembered him suffering a brief episode of the flu, and afterward his attention span went south.

He had known about the toxoplasmosis infection before he'd come; he'd thought he'd be immune. He had no logical reason for believing this, so no surprise that he wasn't.

NutriTopia officials were saying infected people were almost three times as apt to get into a work-related accident, and schizophrenia, hitherto unknown on Mars, was making a comeback as a result of the infection.

The other issue had to do with the need for Martian population growth. Not only were toxoplasmosis-infected women endangering their future offspring's health, they statistically doubled or tripled their chances of bearing a boy rather than a girl.

Lucile suggested this might be NutriTopia's hidden agenda. Because of early immigration practices (only postmenopausal or infertile women were allowed in the initial immigration, due to fears of genetic damage to developing infants), men outnumbered women. A disease that perpetuated that ratio would be unwelcome to the corporations that ruled Mars. That included NutriTopia Ares, which, as Godfrey had pointed out, owned every molecule of Gari Babakin. Mars needs babies. NutriTopia wants more workers.

Life, Lucile believed, was too short to dance with stupid guys, but intelligence was in the eye of the beholder, and she found the infected men of Gari Babakin—Benoît in particular—amusing, if not father-of-her-future-child material.

Of course she was careful not to override the station's contraceptive measures. She didn't want to hurt her theoretical future child.

Godfrey congratulated himself. He had been careful not to take a chance with any of the pastries or cheeses, although they smelled and looked divine. The coffee was hot, so that wasn't a danger, and wine was okay because the oocysts couldn't survive in alcohol.

At least they hadn't offered him any of that raw meat dish, that steak tartare made of hamster meat! How could they—

Headquarters had given Drs. Wrothe and Wriothesley and him very particular instructions about releasing the virus. He was to shake hands with the head elected official, this Jean-Marie Lafayette. Lafayette, his team had discovered, was linked by less than five degrees of separation to every single person on Gari Babakin Station. The virus had been engineered to outlive at least three hand-washings.

Hilda and Kermilda were also to shake hands with as many people as possible, but it seemed the uptight women scientists had been afraid of being infected by the parasite.

He would have to speak to them.

It would work anyway. He had anointed several railings and door handles around that pastry shop and the airlock.

Ah, my my, this Lucile Raoul was a charmer. He had no doubt she was even closer than five degrees of separation from most of the station. He regretted having to return home so precipitously. Oh, to match wits with her!

He also regretted not being able to sample the cheese and pastry. Gari Babakin cuisine was considered exquisite. Their exports to the rest of Mars were irradiated to kill off the oocysts, but two problems remained: one, Martian health officials feared that particularly robust oocysts might live through the irradiation, and the descendants would be harder to kill, thus infecting the entire planet with an unstoppable plague.

Second, the irradiation killed some of the flavor. Godfrey knew this not because he had personally tried a comparison taste test, but because a food scientist from Utopia had done so several Mars years ago, and swore there was no comparison.

That food scientist, one Fred Remaura, had lived in quarantine until recently, when he had been the human test subject for the virus that killed the parasite.

Now, profit motive drove Godfrey's supervisors to sanitize Gari Babakin so that their products would be safe without the flavor-dulling irradiation.

Those little jam tarts—the unaltered fragrance of butter and raspberry jam. And that Rocamadour cheese—yes, yes, very stinky, but what a seductive stink!

Maybe the cheese had some overtones of human sex pheromones.

He smiled at Hilda Wriothesley, but she only shuddered and said, "That woman is a human sewer."

Jean-Marie Lafayette lumbered around the mayor's office, blundering into cabinets and knocking stacks of files off display modules. Every third lap he would haul up in front of Lucile and say, "Do you feel any different? Do I look different?"

"Jean-Marie, just check your biometrics. I don't know if they've even released the virus yet. I don't think we'll know until it's much too late."

"Filthy tight-asses," Benoît was curled in a fetal position in the mayor's desk chair. "They've singled us out for destruction."

Lucile went to him. "Benoît, be wise, poor baby. They are misguided, but they tested the virus on humans, so the damage will probably be minimal. And look at the bright side. Maybe you'll be able to remember the multiplication tables again."

Benoît sprang out of his chair at her, but she smirked her "gotcha" smirk.

Jean-Marie was accessing some database he had suddenly remembered.

"Jean-Marie, darling, turn on your monitor so we can see too."

Jean-Marie tongued on his projector. A scientific paper from some long-forgotten minor Terran journal projected against the wall above the office door.

"Antivirals!" She clasped Jean-Marie's arm joyfully. "But where can we get them?"

Jean-Marie grinned. "Pascal LeBoeuf, our vigneron extraordinaire, my little cabbage."

Hilda tucked her pesticide spray into a pocket in her environment suit and polished the faceplate of her helmet. Godfrey could tell that she was nervous about the passenger cabin in the rocketplane. She preferred to keep her environment suit inflated and her helmet on when she was not inside a clean hab. Her work with infectious diseases had made her paranoid. She hunched in one corner of the cabin, a rodent-like figure of terror, and not touching anything, not even sitting down.

Kermilda, in contrast, believed the best defense was a strong offense, so she had loaded up on so many micronutrients that her breath and scalp emitted a yeasty, alcoholic scent. "They'll figure out right away what we did."

"I don't think so," said Godfrey. "They'll know we started the virus, but they won't know how it's propagated. It won't wash off those yokels' hands, and anyway, I inoculated every surface I encountered in that hab, starting with the mayor's office and even the airlock. And I added a thin layer of the protein substrate."

"Yes," said Kermilda, "but they may try to develop an antiviral."

"That would take time, and by the time they succeed, let's hope they'll come to their senses and realize we have only their greater good in mind." Godfrey contemplated a return to Gari Babakin once this whole thing had blown over. He'd love to meet more of the natives. Especially if any were like that Lucile Raoul. He could write a paper on the personality differences wrought by curing the population of toxoplasmosis infestation. What would Lucile be like when relieved of her parasitic burden? Would she be just as convivial, but not as manipulative?

Hilda spoke for the first time. "I wonder how they'll react when the cats start dying."

Lucile found the half-grown kitten under her workstation when she came in for work. It was cold and limp. She flinched, then cuddled it to her chest. Poor little thing! Poor, poor kitten!

This crystalized her fear that the cats were going to die, all of them. Dozens of pet cats on Gari Babakin Station had already sickened with a mysterious wasting illness, and the feral colony was reduced to a quarter of its former size.

She had been afraid this would happen ever since Godfrey's visit. Jean-Marie had called a town meeting of the entire station. It was the first time that the entire male population had turned up, many of them sober. Everybody knew Godfrey's team would release a virus to kill the oocysts, but there was no way of knowing what method they'd use to propagate it. The water supply had been examined for new viruses, as it was well known that phage virus particles thrive in Earthly sea water, but since Gari Babakin had so few microbiologists who were trained in other than food synthesis, it was like looking for a needle in a haystack.

She threw open the door of Jean-Marie's office. "We've got to take action. They're killing our cats, our souls!"

Jean-Marie rose heavily to his feet and lumbered over to her. He wrapped ham-like arms around her and breathed wine breath into her face. "I know, I know, my dear, but what, what more can we do? We're working on the antivirals—"

"Let me call the head of their sanitation team, that half-scalped idiot that came out here in the spring."

"Is he still on Mars?"

"Of course he is! Earth transport hasn't left Equatorial City since he and his she-goons were here. Anyway, he seems the type that wants to stay on Mars. Become a Martian."

Jean-Marie sighed. "But not a Martian in the truest sense, with the advanced culture provided by our oocyst friends."

"No. Not in the purest sense."

Benoît appeared in the doorway. He was wearing a clean shirt and hadn't crashed the station computer system in weeks. Was the phage destroying his toxoplasmosis infection, converting him back into a straight-arrow Martian?

Benoît said, "You might try seducing him."

"Surely he's not that stupid!"

Benoît stroked his mustache.

Lucile spent more time gazing into Bon Bon's inscrutable eyes, as if the sleek affectionate cat might have answers. A weekly lab test of her own toxoplasmosis status showed that she remained seropositive. The immune factors might just remain in her blood after the cysts were gone. But she thought not. Her bills for package delivery service and droplet manufacturing betrayed her continued interest in exotic lingerie. No, she hadn't started any new love affairs since the fateful day Godfrey and his hagfish entourage had arrived, but she had been busy. Anyway, her next project was Benoît.

Or was it?

Benoît would make an interesting playmate. He would need lots of fixing up, but toxoplasmosis-positive women liked that sort of thing. Of course, toxoplasmotic women also got bored easily.

She needed more of a challenge. Terrans were certainly not immune to the charms of women with toxoplasmosis infections; this was well known. Many of the station women had a good laugh when one of them seduced another male into coming to the station on the sheer expectation of meeting the famed Gari Babakin sex kittens.

This particular challenge might save the station.

She put through the call.

Dr. Godfrey Worcester, NutriTopia Ares Project Manager for *Toxoplasma gondii* Remediation, was in fact still on Mars, at Utopia Station. And, his expression told her, even on her tiny screen, that he was both lonely and shy, but too damned dutiful to admit it to himself.

"Do I have the honor of speaking to the too-young-to-be-so-distinguished Dr. Godfrey Worcester? The scientist who developed the anti-toxoplasma virus?"

"Martialle Raoul, good sol," he said. He sounded courteous, but nervous. As he should be.

She made her voice soft and breathy, as if afraid she might wet her pants in admiration. "I have been thinking of you ever since you left us that day. We had so much to talk about."

He brightened. "I was actually hoping to see you again, Martialle Raoul—"

She method-acted her face into an expression of fetching grief, combined with vixenish fury. "My naughty doctor," she said in low, thrilling voice, "are you aware that you're killing our little kitties?"

He wilted like a failed erection. "We—uh, we considered there might be side effects with the cats. But surely not all—"

"Seventy percent! That includes Aristide Brewpub, the tom cherished by our mayor. Aristide died in agony a week after your visit. Autopsy shows kidney and heart failure, caused by the sudden death of the oocysts that the cat coexisted with." Actually, Aristide was perfectly well, but several other pet cats had died, and she figured Godfrey would be more appalled if he thought he'd killed the mayor's cat.

"There's nothing—uh, our own feline subjects tolerated the phage very well—"

She closed her eyes slowly, as if infinitely offended.

He blurted, "Are you experiencing any discomfort? I mean

personally? I could come to the station and examine you. I'm a physician, you know. I don't want you to feel in peril with this perfectly safe treatment."

"Don't you understand, my dear bad, bad doctor? We love our cats. They are, how shall I say? The soul of our culture."

"But some of them are running around without masters, infesting your vacant tunnels—"

"You mean the feral cat community?" She blinked slowly at him. "On Earth, I believe there are actually more wild animals than domestic. We have reproduced that condition in miniature here in Gari Babakin." She leaned forward, pursed her lips. "I have an idea. I think you should come, as my guest of course, and experience firsthand this culture your corporate masters condemn."

Godfrey blanched. "You mean allow myself to be infected with toxoplasmosis? I'm afraid that's out of the—"

"But not at all! Your virus has wiped out the oocysts. The death of all our sweet pusskins shows that to be true. Come, you can stay in our charming little guesthouse. You'll be perfectly safe. Or with me, if you like."

Surely, he's not that stupid.

But he was nodding yes. Eagerly.

Godfrey's head was spinning when he turned off the call. She wanted to see him. Of course his motive was entirely scientific. He wanted to check the progress of the cure. Were the personality changes going to be obvious? His team had been monitoring internal and external communications from Gari Babakin for seven years. Text analysis, algorithm driven, had demonstrated marked deviation from normalcy. But he had actually met three victims of the disease: the mayor Jean-Marie Lafayette; Benoît Bussy, the mayor's research liaison; and of course the mayor's interesting assistant, Lucile.

He would be able to see firsthand if her personality had

changed. Had she become less obsessed with fashion and personal appearance? That outfit she was wearing the sol he had been there—provocative, in a way he couldn't describe. Was she less effusive? Most of all, had she been cured of that regrettable promiscuity suggested by her secret smile?

The cure for promiscuity was without question the best feature of the virus cure. Except maybe for saving infants from blindness and encephalitis. And yet! She was interested in him; he could see from the look in her violet eyes that she wanted to see him. Perhaps—

He wasn't interested in romancing an experimental subject. Of course not.

He just wanted to see how the treatment (don't call it an experiment!) had turned out.

From ground level.

Of course if she and he decided to see each other socially, after the experiment was over—

The danger of becoming infected with toxoplasmosis was vanishingly small now, according to the computer model of how his virus cure had spread. And if he did become infected, he could just use the virus cure on himself.

A rocketplane was scheduled to go to Gari Babakin on Thursday. He would be aboard.

Plenty of time for him to make an appointment with his barber.

Lucile liked scientists. Since they spent most of their time with their eyes glued to a microscope or a computer output, they lacked the social lubrication of the public servants in the circles she moved in. Scientists were often charmingly direct. Unsophisticated, in the sense of lacking sophistry. She wasn't sure where this would go, but it would be no great chore flirting with Godfrey until she got whatever information she could out of him.

This time, she flinched inwardly when he took off his helmet. His scalp showed through in two places where the barber had apparently not been paying attention. But his eager smile, along with his scent of clean sweat, melted her heart.

"Now," he said, "let's discuss this issue with the feline side effects."

She took his helmet from him, helped him with the fasteners on his suit. "Where are your two associates, by the way?"

"They had other commitments."

Lucile repressed a smile. But of course. He hadn't even told them he was coming.

Less than twenty-four and a half hours later, they were in Lucile's bed, eating foie gras that Étienne Bergere had grown from duck liver cells. Lucile was always hungry after she consummated a seduction.

"You are not going back to the guest house tonight," she told him as he licked the last morsels off her fingers. "I can order breakfast in tomorrow morning. Shall I speak the lights out?"

They settled into the bed. Lucile was always a bit uncomfortable sleeping with a new partner, but the bed was big, and she did like Godfrey. He'd let go a few of the secrets of the virus, including calling up a genomic profile from Marsnet. It was proprietary, but he had a password and went into NutriTopia Ares's file system. She'd copied it and tucked a duplicate into her own private files.

The wonderful thing was, she could just sit back and not do anything.

Mars itself would do the work.

Lucile was pleasantly dozing when she heard Bon Bon hacking up a hairball on the carpet. The coughing went on too long to be just a hairball. Bon Bon had been extra affectionate lately. Cats with kidney issues often sought the heat of human flesh. She switched on a light.

Bon Bon was convulsing on the floor by her bed. As she watched in horror, the little cat quivered one last time, then lay still.

Without answering Godfrey's sleepy "What's wrong?" she scooped the cat up, bundled on a trench coat, and ran to the emergency medical clinic.

The medico on duty worked on the little cat for over twenty minutes, but it was quite dead.

"The virus?" she said.

The medico washed off her handfilm and shook her head. "Poor little thing. We think it may be like heart-worms: kill the parasite, kill the host."

Lucile was more than horrified. Her cat, her companion for eight Mars years, which had listened to her secrets and mirrored her slinking and her primping like a tiny mime, was cooling on a clinic table.

"Are you saying it could kill humans?" This was a nightmare!

At this point she realized that Godfrey had fumbled into his clothes and followed her to the clinic.

"No, no, no," said Godfrey. "The human test was completely successful! No ill effects whatever."

She turned on him with the fury of a global storm. "Then what killed my cat?"

He smiled unconvincingly. "It has to do with taurine enzymes. Uh, I don't think you'd understand—"

Oh, she was furious. "Try me!"

He buttoned one more button of his shirt. "The thing is, nobody completely understands it. We just know it works, because of the enzyme-blocking, you see."

The clinic medico said, "It's not really a parasite, like other protozoans. When a parasite evolves long enough with a species, it is no longer useful for it to kill the host. It eventually offers benefits to the host. When rats eat cat feces, the rats become infected. The rats' brains are changed. We think it might emulate a dopamine reuptake inhibitor. The rats begin to love cats. They are even attracted to the smell of cat urine."

"And this helps the cat." Lucile stroked the fur of her dead Bon Bon, who seemed asleep with half-open eyes. "Godfrey, how does the virus work? How do you know it won't kill everybody on this station? Even you!"

"The discovery was an accident. We were looking for a bacteriophage for a different disease."

She lowered her voice an octave and stalked closer to him. "How does the virus work?"

He backed away. "We—aren't sure."

She sank down on her heels on the floor of the clinic and buried her face in her hands, unconcerned that her coat gapped open and revealed her nudity underneath. She looked up at Godfrey and said, "You have killed my cat."

"I didn't—"

"Something was wrong. You must have known."

"All right!" he barked. "All right! We didn't test it on cats! We tested it on hamsters because hamsters are cheaper. Hamsters are like cats, aren't they? Small, furry, warm-blooded? And we tested it on Fred Remaura, and he did just fine."

Lucile could barely contain her fury. "This is really true? You tested this virus on hamsters and one man, and then you unleashed it on two thousand innocent people and—oh my God —we have over five thousand cats here."

"I'm sorry," he said meekly.

"You'll be sorrier," she said with icy calm, "if you're not off this station tonight. Within the hour."

"I can't—there's no rocketplane until—"

"So call Utopia for emergency evacuation. No, wait, I'll call Jean-Marie. We have a rocketplane we use for light delivery. It isn't pressurized, so you'll have to stay suited up the whole flight, but I won't have to look at your lying face tomorrow. Or ever."

Godfrey got all stiff. "You forget that NutriTopia Ares owns every molecule of this station, right down to—"

"And this is relevant how?"

"I am a stockholder in NutriTopia Ares! I have rights here."

"How delightful for you! But it won't do you much good if you're here beyond tomorrow morning."

Godfrey deflated. "Why not?"

"Because you'll be dead."

He backed off, shaking his head and staring at her. She locked eyes with him until he turned and fled.

She stroked the still body of Bon Bon and wept.

She told Jean-Marie, "The feral cats will save us. They inhabit the upper tunnels, where there is less protection from surface radiation. We have to do everything we can to ensure that some survive."

They fed and watered the feral cats. The cats died by the dozens, the hundreds. But Lucile, Benoît, and Jean-Marie fed them and took the bodies away.

Jean-Marie's cat Aristide Brewpub did die. And so did the cats Benoît kept, Coeurl and her kittens, Albedo One and Chimère, rare albinos.

Lucile herself went through a horrible patch, ill with headaches and jaundice. ("Been hitting the wine a bit much, Lucile?" Benoît had fleered, and then she had whacked him on the shoulder with her expandable office.) She checked herself once more for toxoplasmosis, and the test said she was still positive, but a more expensive test, ordered from Utopia, said no, she was clear of the oocysts. She threw into the recycler silky heaps of expensive lingerie and stiletto-heeled boots with built-in gyro stabilizers to prevent a twisted ankle. She mourned the woman she had been.

How could she have enjoyed being the slave of that microscopic tyrant, the puppet of that parasite? How tragic to be human, to ride the waves of passion steered by the wayward blood. Who was the real Lucile, the manic flirt, in love with color, self-adornment, and complex flavors on the tongue, or the sad rational woman cured of her infection?

Benoît did indeed remember the multiplication tables again, and proved to be such a finicky organizer of her life and Jean-Marie's that she could barely tolerate the glare of clean desk surfaces.

She wanted a kitten. She wanted to be sexy. She didn't want sex, she just wanted to be crazy and attractive again.

She wanted to be a kitten.

It took an entire Mars year for the die-offs to cease.

But.

As hard as it was, Lucile and the others had only one weapon: time.

Time, and the extreme environment of Mars.

The very harsh environment that forced the people of Gari Babakin to live under meters of regolith proved to be their friend.

It was just as she had learned from the notes in the Nutri-Topia Ares files.

Toxoplasma gondii was a protozoan similar to *Plasmodium*, the parasite that, on Earth, causes malaria. The difficulty of wiping out malaria on Earth is that the protozoan keeps mutating, so a drug that works one year will lose its efficacy a few years later. The protozoan mutates, develops immunity. On Earth, *Toxoplasma gondii* never did this, maybe because there was never a concerted effort to wipe it out.

But more likely it was because on Earth, *Toxoplasma gondii* didn't mutate very fast.

Mars organisms, all of them, are bathed in constant cosmic

radiation. The radiation speeds mutations, and most of these are harmful. But if you're a parasite, and you reproduce very fast—

So they had only one solution: to take very good care of the cats in the upper tunnels, where the mutations would occur fastest.

The best meat. Carefully formulated meals, with plenty of taurine. Clean water always available, from cat-sized drinking fountains.

"We must be very brave now," whispered Lucile. She squeezed the hands of Benoît and Jean-Marie.

———

At the end of a Mars year—such a long time!—Lucile roused herself to take Benoît and Jean-Marie up to the tunnels where they had been cosseting the feral cats.

The cats looked different this time. Many of them had been dull-coated and listless the previous times they had visited. Today, there were fewer cats—so many had crawled away to die, and would have to be found and cremated—but those remaining were sleek and lively, fleeing the humans, or turning on them, puffing up with hisses and growls.

Lucile cornered one and picked it up to examine. It struggled fiercely, but she gripped its back paws and soothed it with her free hand. Then she peered closely into its eyes. Its mucosa were pink and unblemished, its fear and fury palpable signs of health.

She clipped one of its claws too short and harvested a blood sample to take back to the lab.

It snarled and would have bitten her but for her quick reflexes. She let it go and it streaked away, leaving claw marks on her arms. But she smiled.

Benoît caught her hand up and licked away her blood.

"All we had to do was take care that some of them survived," she said.

———

The cats were hard to count, but the estimate was that thirty cats were still alive on Gari Babakin Station.

And the one Lucile had tested bore toxoplasmosis oocysts.

Which meant that they probably all did.

And those oocysts now contained *Toxoplasma gondii* that were immune to Godfrey's virus.

The surviving feral cats were reproducing. Godfrey Worcester hadn't dared come back to the station, but he had sent Dr. Hilda Wriothesley and Dr. Kermilda Wrothe, who wrung their hands and scolded, but since cats are easy to hide, they didn't have much wind in their sails, and besides, there was an outbreak of athlete's foot in Argyre Planitia City.

Nobody from NutriTopia Ares apologized, and Lucile nurtured a small cold emerald of hatred in her heart.

Benoît gave her a tiny kitten. It clung to his shirt until he detached each of its twenty-four claws and handed it to Lucile.

"Where did you get it?"

He raised his eyebrows.

"It has a name?"

"I offer you that honor."

"Éclair," she decided. Éclair sank its twenty-four tiny needles into the fabric of her jumpsuit and purred. Its body was very warm. Its tongue was very pink.

"The feral cat colony is back in force." Benoît tried not to smirk.

"I thought everybody would take all the remaining cats for pets, after most of them died."

He shrugged. "Not all cats agree to be pets, just as not all Martians agree to play kiss-ass with the corporate jackboots.

Some old toms fought like tigers. They don't trust humans, after what happened."

"And they all have toxoplasmosis? The virus has run its course?"

"Apparently. And people are eating raw meat again. They're raising hamsters to make steak tartare, imagine that."

She smiled slowly. "What a scandal."

The medico at the clinic which had failed to revive Bon Bon had theories of her own. On Earth, toxoplasmosis benefited cats because cats were the top predator in their environment. Humans didn't count in that environment, because they didn't prey on either cats or rats. But on Mars—well, certain humans could be top predators. At least, the mutated toxoplasmosis seemed to foster that situation.

But their prey was other humans, those of a different genetic background, in a suave and civilized way. Because NutriTopia Ares failed to understand that the virus hadn't completely wiped out toxoplasmosis, it spread wherever food was shipped from Gari Babakin.

Those with these secondary infections, with the other genomic background, behaved like prey animals. Prey animals that don't die, but rather buy. They were infatuated with all the products of Gari Babakin culture.

"We are the Paris of Mars," Lucile said. She twirled, enjoying the swirl of her new red frock. Benoît and she had designed it, and now she was modeling it for a test audience: him and Jean-Marie. Soon she would offer it, as she had other creations, to the wealthy of Mars. Benoît had a flair for design, it turned out, though she didn't trust him to keep the Chez Raoul company books. She hired a woman for that.

She did, however, trust Benoît to father a child. The two designers did not breathe entirely easily until the little boy had reached his second birthsol and showed no damage from toxoplasmosis.

Étienne LeBouef had opened a small restaurant that required reservations a Mars year in advance. A mysterious vigneron now bottled a wine so exquisite that Terran billionaires paid huge sums to have it shipped to them on Earth.

Dr. Hilda Wriothesley and Dr. Kermilda Wrothe won Mars Global Storm Awards for their work in protozoan dopamine metabolism. Lucile watched the ceremony via netlink.

"Oh, look, Tigercat," she said to Benoît, "they're wearing knockoffs of our gowns."

Benoît, busy composing a poison pen letter to the Prime Minister of Key West, wasn't watching. "How do you know they're knockoffs?"

"Darling, we'd know if orders had been placed. And neither of them can afford originals. But more to the point, look at how they drape. Droplet manufacturing can't even approximate the real thing, eh?"

Dr. Godfrey Worcester, sadly, found himself unable to do serious science after his collaboration with Drs. Wrothe and Wriothesley. He disappeared. Rumor had it he was deported to Earth after his arrest for stalking Lucile Raoul.

He said he loved her.

ALEX

WHEN THE TIME *comes round again, She leaves her throne, walks down from Heaven, and hearkens to mortal longings.*

Cara paced in the patch of sunshine on her linoleum floor, cell phone mashed to her ear.

"Tell me you didn't," her friend Judith shrilled on the other end. "You met this guy at an Italian American club dance, and you invite him over. This is smart? This is safe? Cara, do you watch the news?"

"This is not a blind date," said Cara. "He comes to the dances at least once a month, and I've seen him at Vitello's Deli. Name's Alex Cacciato. He wrote his telephone number on a napkin—"

"Which you mysteriously can't find."

"It's in my car. I thought I put it in my bag, but it must be in my car." Actually, Cara had ransacked her VW Rabbit, even under the floor mats and in the seat cracks. But the guy had to be okay. Lived in the neighborhood, Mayfield and Murray Hill, Little Italy. Her territory. A local, or maybe one of the artist types who were moving in, seeking low-rent studios.

"Cara, don't let him in. Say you're sick and don't let him in."

Cara took the phone away from her ear and took three calming breaths. Then she returned it to her mouth. "Judith, I'm thirty-three. The ol' Timex battery is running down. If I'm going to—you know—"

"Get married. Say it."

"—to have a lover, or even any fun, I need to risk. This morning I found a spider vein on the back of my leg. Listen, he has this sexy mustache. Green eyes. Buns to die for. He's so cute—"

"So was Ted Bundy."

Cara rubbed her finger around the edge of the phone, torn. Judith had been her friend throughout library school, but Judith lacked Cara's earthy touch. The minute Judith had landed a job, she had moved into a singles complex on Lake Erie. Cara had kept her old-fashioned apartment in Little Italy. Sure, Cara could afford a new place, but she liked the patch of sun on the kitchen linoleum, the claw-foot tub in the bathroom, the jungle of spider-plants she raised on the porch, the landlord's indifference to her ginger tomcat.

Should she let Judith talk her out of the date? Alex was due—oh, God, now!

Judith said, "Don't let him in. If he's legit, he'll call again—"

"What if he doesn't? I can't let this one slip away! After Gene—"

"Gene tried to run over your cat."

"An accident. Also, cats aggravated his Borna-Tupaia syndrome."

"Gene was a rat. Dumped you because he found a cat hair in his carrot juice."

Cara felt glum. "The guy probably won't turn up, anyway."

"He might. Creeps flock to you like rats to garbage. No, that's mean. I meant flies to honey."

Cara felt even worse. She looked at her nails, painted two different colors because Claws von Pumpkin had batted the

Porcelain Pinkie off the dresser, forcing her to finish with Iceberry Slink. "Gotta be some nice guys out there."

"But you keep ending up with vermin. You're a masochist, girl."

Judith was right. Of course, Judith didn't date, but she read many books about relationships, such as *How to Find an Almost Nice Guy* and *Men Who Make Fun of Women and How to Embarrass Them.*

"Judith, I gotta do it. There were sparks. Chemistry."

Judith paused, and Cara figured she was lighting a cigarette. "Yeah, chemistry. As in chemical warfare."

The phone felt hot, slippery as a vibrator that had been running too long.

The doorbell rang.

Without saying goodbye, Cara hung up.

Morituri te salutamus.

He was just as hot as she had remembered. Copper-colored chest hair peeked out above the buttons of his denim shirt. "Alex! I hope you're not allergic," said Cara, opening the door wide. "I'm sorry my apartment is so—"

"Just like my place." Alex squeezed past her into the kitchen.

Shit. Had she left that burned pan in the sink? Had Claws von Pumpkin left a giant turd in the litter box? Not really sure Alex would keep the date, she had tidied up only halfheartedly.

Thank God Claws von P. was outdoors. He always got friendly with visitors who were violently allergic.

Cara scurried after Alex. Oh, shit! Slimy chicken skin in the sink drainer! Smelly tuna in the cat dish! And Alex was peeking into the refrigerator.

"It's not, um, quite ready."

"That's okay. Just wondered what we were having."

Oh no! With her luck, he was a vegetarian! He was sort of on the thin side. Wiry, really.

Nice build.

Now, Cara, she scolded, *going to bed with this strange man right away would be dangerous.*

But lots of fun.

"You're a vegetarian?" she asked.

He shuddered. "Only if force-fed." He moved bottles around in the refrigerator. Made himself right at home. Still—so cute. Thick auburn hair, green eyes. His jeans hugged his butt so nicely, and the blue shirt stretched over his shoulder blades.

"Nice shirt," she said.

"Thank you. I borrowed it, and guess what? There was a twenty in the pocket." He leaned toward her and inhaled. "Mm, smells good."

Had she turned the oven too high? "Chicken."

He yawned. "Not me. I'm pretty bold. How about you?"

He brushed his cheek against her hair. She caught a woodsy scent, clean, but not out of a bottle.

He leaned over and tickled her neck with his mustache. Immediately, she felt her panties get wet.

Judith, she thought, *see what a slut I am?*

In a tiny voice, she said, "You're going too fast."

Alex stepped back and, looking confused, smoothed his mustache.

Lady crowned with hawthorn, Mistress of the white owl, Beloved of the Day Lord, listen to our pleadings.

Alex ate neatly, eyes narrowed with enjoyment, avoiding the broccoli. And he had three helpings of ice cream. "So what do you do when you're not at home?" he asked.

"I'm a bibliothecary."

"You are not! You're a librarian."

And Alex? He told her he worked in security. She relaxed. How could he be a mass murderer? He told anecdotes about the evil dog who lived with the Russos, her downstairs neighbors, then gazed at her with dreamy interest. Suddenly he said, "Did you see that *Now You See It* episode where they made people think animals were talking?"

"I like it when they serve people weird food in restaurants."

He sniffed her daisy centerpiece. "Claws von Pumpkin is a stupid name for a cat."

"Big orange tom—what else would I call him? Maybe 'Screwdriver'?"

"Sandy," said Alex. "You should call him Sandy. Or Red."

"He won't answer, whatever I call him."

"Cats have feelings. They're very intelligent."

"Sure, I suppose they learn their letters and numbers, from watching Sesame Street."

He licked his ice cream spoon. "And now what?"

Her hormones screamed, *Take him! Take him!*

A wiser voice said, *Screw him on the first date and you'll never see him again.*

So she opened the newspaper to the movie schedule.

They saw a show about sharks and jewel thieves. Alex enjoyed the movie so much his eyes glittered. In the quiet parts, when sharks weren't eating people and thieves weren't grabbing the Koh-i-noor diamond, he caressed Cara's ear with the tip of his tongue, getting her amethyst earring damp.

She liked that.

Turn Your bright face upon us, Lady, for our hearts are breaking.

At the door, Cara had a flashbulb epiphany. Alex wouldn't call her again. He would disappear, because that was the way men were. Easily bored. For some reason, men only enjoyed one-night stands. If she went to bed with him, he would fade like last summer's suntan. But if she didn't, he would still disappear.

Not only did men not stay with the same woman, they also never got married. Only women got married, not men.

All this stuff in the media about both sexes getting married was just PR for the wedding industry. That was why newspapers never printed the photo of the groom, just the bride. When it was necessary to show both bride and groom, they hired a model.

Children were not really produced by couples. They were decanted in a baby-farm in Akron and given false memories of childhood.

Her friend Judith was right. A relationship was not in the cards.

Still, Alex was hot. As long as he was going to dump her anyway, she deserved one night of bliss.

"Hey, Alex, how about another dish of ice cream?"

He followed her into the apartment, went into the bedroom, and sprawled on the bed.

"Bashful, aren't you?" she said.

Alex looked confused. "Didn't you want—?" He started to rise, but she flung herself on him.

They rolled around, nibbling each other's lips, ears, and necks.

He stroked her neck, then attacked the buttons on her blouse, nails catching on the silk.

"Let me," she whispered. He watched her undo the zippers and buttons, his eyes half-closed with sensuality.

She stroked his luxuriant bronze body hair, then brushed herself against him. He leaned into her caress, exciting her.

"Yes! A screamer," he said.

In the night, twice, he woke her, nipping the back of her neck. It was lovely.

"Don't leave me," she moaned.

"Oh, I'll be back, in a while." He slipped out of bed. She waited, expecting to hear the toilet flush or the shower run. At length, exhausted and satiated, she dozed off.

———

Lady whose substance is light, You change all things. Longing or fulfilled, the wisest of us honor You.

———

And in the morning, Sunday morning, Alex was gone.

He won't call, of course, she told herself, and moped around in a ragged chenille robe, slurping coffee and watching Galaxy Queen.

She went through her purse again and found the napkin with Alex's number on it.

The creep!

He had written her number on it.

And yet—he had been delicious. And he used condoms without being asked. Call the whole thing an adventure, almost risk-free.

Still another part of her thought, *He was sexy, so engagingly direct. If only he would come back, just once!*

Toward noon, the doorbell rang.

Cara threw off the old robe and sprinted for the closet. Her red satin kimono wasn't too wrinkled. She threw it on, kicked off the beat-up loafers, fluffed her hair. Makeup? No time! She slapped her cheeks in lieu of rouge and opened the door.

Aw, shit.

Judith stood outside, with Claws von Pumpkin draped over one arm.

Judith said, "Look what I found in the basement, lying on the Russo's clean laundry again. And he had a dead rat."

"It's just you," said Cara, defeated.

"Don't tell me you slept with that Alex guy!"

"Judith, shut up."

"What could I expect? Last night was the full moon."

Claws von Pumpkin jumped out of Judith's arms, rubbed his muzzle against Cara's ankles, and sauntered into the bedroom. On the bed stand was the melted remains of Alex's fifth dish of ice cream.

Purring avidly, Claws licked the dish.

Back in the living room, he settled on Cara's lap to watch *Spiderman, Meerkat Manor,* and, later, *Now You See It.* In this episode an actor impersonated an exterminator.

Lady of Light, avatar of Bast, in the dark of each cycle we await the return of Your power.

NEFERTITI'S TENTH LIFE

I LAY on the cold table while my slaves petted me. Water dripped from their faces. Evil smells, dog piss and antiseptic fluid, made my whiskers twitch feebly.

My female slave said, "And it will purr, and have fur, just like Nefertiti?"

And the bad doctor said, "It will *be* Nefertiti. It won't be just a mechanical cat. It will have her Siamese meow, all her little tricks, her raspy tongue, her whiskers. Everything that makes a cat a cat. Except she'll be younger, like when she was a kitten. And you can pet her, and play cat and mouse games with her."

My man slave said, "What about catnip?"

"That's a little more complicated. You'll have to say 'catnip' The sensors aren't attuned to odors, although they're working on that. It's possible you could get it installed later, when they bring out a new model."

"It's so hard to let her go."

The bad doctor said, "It's normal for you to grieve. But really, she'll just go to sleep—and wake up in a new, more permanent body."

They snuffled awhile.

"Shall I leave you two with her for a while?"

"No, no, we're ready. We just—wanted to know what to expect."

"This is the end of all her pain." But it wasn't quite. There was a claw-prick in my neck, and then things stopped hurting, one by one. The ache in my back legs. The feeling that I had to piss all the time, even when nothing would come out. The heaviness in my chest. The burning in my gut. And I slept.

When I wake up, I am lying on the slaves' bed, which is where I like to nap. Lately, I have not been strong enough to leap up. They made the bed too high for me. Slaves do things like that.

I forget what woke me up. Maybe the screaming of the two women who live next door, the young one who is just old enough to compete for males and the old shrill one. I got used to it before, so I didn't notice it. Or maybe my hearing is better now.

I yawn, and stretch, and lick my fur. My fur has no taste, but I lick it anyway, to get good and clean after the bad doctor's office. Then I hop off the bed and saunter down to where the slaves are watching their television. Yorick, my big yellow dog, is lying on the floor in his usual place. He opens his yellow eyes, sniffs me without interest, and goes back to sleep.

I let them watch television in the evening, because it keeps them busy when I'm occupied with other things.

But I don't want them to get the idea they can get up and do something else when I want them. I pad over to the female slave and leap toward her lap.

But accidentally (am I so strong, now?), I leap past her and hit the table with the lamp. It crashes down, and she jumps up to straighten it. Yorick stumbles to his feet, ready to bark. He's the one that usually knocks things over. He's stupid, like most dogs, even less trainable than the human slaves, but nice to sleep next to on a cold evening.

My slave picks me up and puts me on her lap.

I don't like the slaves to get the idea they are allowed to decide when to pick me up, but when her hands go round my chest and under my shanks, I feel a deep tingle of pleasure. *PLEASURE!* So I let her settle me in her lap and begin to purr and knead as she strokes the fur on my back.

She says, "Does the fur feel different from Nefertiti's? Come pet her and see."

The male slave gets up and strokes me. *PLEASURE.*

The female says, "Maybe it is the same. Nefertiti was so silky."

"The vet said this is Nefertiti. We have to learn to think of her that way. She doesn't look all that different."

"I guess. Her eyes are the same."

"She's a lot heavier, though. Warm. But solid, as if I were stroking a bean bag covered with sable."

I purr.

"Shall we try the catnip?"

At this, I suddenly feel my whole body go wild with excitement. Catnip! The word sends me into rapture!

I spring out of her lap and carom around the room. I am a kitten again! I give a playful slap at the floor lamp and knock it over. Then I notice the drapes. I haven't climbed up to the top of the room for years and years!

From a running start, I vault up and begin to climb. What ecstasy! Up and up! I claw my way toward the ceiling—

—and suddenly the whole drapery sways and pulls out and I am falling backward, away from the wall in a wild arc. A wall of fabric and a big heavy rod slap down atop me with a *whump*. Trapped! I writhe and struggle, batting at the heavy shroud. Yorick barks madly, and the slaves yell and swear.

Then, salvation! The slaves pull the material off me, and I streak upstairs. Back to the slaves' bed, and under it.

I stay there a long time, listening to the screaming of the women next door. The old one screams, "You're a slut! You don't deserve to live!" The young one says, "Don't, please! You'll hurt the baby!"

My slaves come upstairs. I stay under the bed. They sleep and wake and sleep, night and day, three times, and in between they ask, "Kitty, kitty, kitty?" with their big moon faces peering upside down at me, and I just glare.

"Won't she get hungry?" asks the male slave. "I know they don't eat, but Nefertiti was always such a creature of routine. She'll miss the morning and evening ritual."

"I don't know. I'm tempted to say the C word, just to get her out. But maybe we should let her get used to her new body."

"We could call the vet."

When they get out of bed the fourth day, I make up my mind. The drapery thing was a mistake, and I can stop it from happening again. I am strong now, and maybe I have gained some weight. Cats sometimes do that. It's true, I feel no real hunger, but maybe I can get them to put down some of that smelly stuff out of the cans.

They are pitifully happy to see me. The female slave says, "Oh, it's Nefertiti. It truly is! I can believe it now."

And the male takes that complicated thing with gears and levers and cuts off the top of the can. He puts down just a taste of the stuff on a saucer.

I walk over and sniff it. It has no smell. They have done something to the food. Or they bought the wrong kind. But I wasn't hungry anyway. I lift my tail and walk away.

"Yorick will eat it," says the female slave.

"I hope so. Cat food is pretty expensive to keep up a charade like this."

But Yorick is already at the saucer, finishing all of it in one big lick.

What nerve. I walk over and swat his wet, snotty nose, just to teach him his place.

To my surprise, Yorick flies across the room and cowers whimpering at the foot of the dishwasher.

My slaves both go to Yorick and pet him and feel his nose. The female gets a paper towel and holds it to his snotty nose, and it comes away red. The red might be blood, but I can't smell it, so I don't know. It might be paint.

They spend a long time with him, ignoring me. I wash myself, but my fur is still quite tasteless. Very clean, I imagine. I've always been very clean. That's what my slaves say.

"I thought you said the thing was declawed," says the male, looking at me with a look I don't quite like.

"They never said, but I thought so." They both come at me and I bristle.

"Maybe just the force of the blow. What is it made of?"

"Metal and plastic, mostly, I suppose. It's heavy enough." She comes at me with hate in her eyes. Human faces are easy to read if you are a cat. "Bad kitty! Bad! You mustn't hurt Yorick!"

I run. They both chase me, and I run and hide under their bed again.

But I am lonely. I remember the rush of *PLEASURE* when the female slave held me, so when they are both good and asleep, I spring up onto the bed, as lightly as I can. I used to be able to do that, long ago, without waking them up. But then when I was sick, I couldn't manage to get up off the floor at all, and just sat there, meowing pitifully in that tone that always gets to humans. This time, I land too hard, and they wake up.

But the female just says, "Hi, Nefertiti. You ready to cuddle?" And they both go back to sleep.

The two women next door do not scream tonight. I settle between the male slave's feet, a nice warm place, and the *PLEA-SURE* comes back, rich and strong, and I purr and purr and purr and never think any more about the screaming women, or my yellow dog Yorick, who sleeps outside the door because they don't let him in the bedroom.

I hear Yorick whimper in his sleep. Maybe he dreams. Maybe he dreams that he could chastise a large Siamese cat.

In the night, the male slave thrashes and turns over. He does that. It's in human nature; they are imperfect sleepers.

But he kicks me. I complain, mildly, of course. He's just a human, he can't help it.

But he yells as if I had bitten him. "Damn thing is like a brick! I think I broke my toe."

"Well," says the female sleepily. "Maybe you shouldn't have kicked her."

But the next night, they take me off the bed and close the door. I have to sleep in the hall, with the drooling, stupid yellow dog.

I have my humans, and I have no pain, and I am strong. But somehow things are not right. The humans flinch away from me when I rub their ankles. There is a thing the humans call love, and I feel it is missing now. Before, even when I was sick and dying, there was love, and now it has flowed away. There is the PLEASURE when one of them picks me up, and still more PLEA-SURE when I hop into their laps, where they still let me stay when they watch their television.

But something is missing in my humans.

I decide I will forget them. I need a good hunt. I scratch the door to get outside and chase birds, but the male says, "Suppose she gets wet. Won't the chassis get rusty?"

"She's supposed to be durable. The fur is drip-dry. We're supposed to wash her once a week, or whenever she gets dirty."

Like a dog. As if I couldn't keep myself clean.

But they won't let me out.

One day, from across the room, I watch a cardinal throw itself stupidly against the glass. The impact stuns it, but it flaps up and does it again. And again. Bastet gave birds wings to compensate for their incredible lack of intellect. But this cardinal (a male) clearly is so stupid it should be prevented from siring chicks. I know there is glass between me and that feather-brain, but somehow—is it because my female slave had the windows washed yesterday?—I forget there is a pane between me and the silly morsel.

I retreat a dozen paces from the window, then turn, then crouch, stock still. Wait until the bird recovers from its latest collision. From a distance, I focus my whole being on that scarlet flash. I waggle my hindquarters, and I launch.

The glass shatters against my nose, and I seize the pea-brained mouthful. It squawks and flutters. Feathers brilliant as blood fly around me. Ecstasy!

I pad to the porch and lie down to disassemble my treasure. The guts are slick and long, and I pull them eagerly from the twitching body.

But I'm not hungry. I remember the smell of bird blood, juicy and hot, but this bird is tasteless and without aroma.

I can, of course, use it as a hostess gift to my slaves, in recompense for their recent acts of service, and maybe get them to love me again, too. So, bearing the bright treasure in my mouth, I leap back through the window, avoiding glittering shards that might damage my fur.

It happens that the female slave is home alone, gazing mindlessly at a heap of paper in her lap. I land beside her, and she screams.

I've heard her scream before when I bring her gifts, and I attribute her shrieks to excessive excitement. After all, she could never actually catch a bird as I can, and she never gets really fresh meat. Her mate and she sometimes bring stale, cold meat into the house and eat it. And then there's the matter of the somewhat rotten cooked meat that comes in the little cans.

"Bad! Bad kitty!" she screams.

Then it dawns on me. She is upset that I have broken the window.

But it is my house. How can she object?

When the male comes home, the two of them call a dirty-looking man in coveralls to put in a new pane of glass. I see cat and dog hairs on the legs of his pants, but sniff as I can, I can't detect their odors.

"I think we should let her out," says my male slave.

The female says nothing. She just opens the door. I look at the open door. It is bad to let your humans believe that they can control when you come and go, but the autumn sunshine lures me. I saunter out.

And I stay out. I chase leaves and birds and chipmunks and a dog. The dog is a bully of a German Shepherd who belongs to the older of the two screaming women next door. It used to snarl and bar my way when I was weaker.

It barks at me once. When I puff out my fur, it crouches down menacingly and growls.

So I leap on it and bury my teeth in its snout.

It twists and tries to roll me off, but I am clever and strong, and I hold on. I ride it halfway into its own back yard before I become bored with it and let it go.

It is way too big to eat.

No, I am not really tired tonight. I never seem to tire since I recovered from my illness. But I grow curious about my humans. And also perhaps lonely.

So I climb the tree outside my humans' window. I know that tree goes to their window. I can see it every night from their bed, and there is a little red play-disk that someone has tossed up and which is stuck in it. So it is easy to find.

I wait until they come in and take off their outer skins, as humans do. It always seems curious that they have these extra skins, and I like very much to smell them and then perhaps settle down and sleep on them. They lie in the bed and wrestle for a while, the kind of wrestling that I think has something to do with mating, only there are never any kittens, so I don't know. Perhaps their previous cat had them fixed.

After, the male says, "We should let the cat in."

"I don't know. She hasn't tried to get back in. Maybe she ran away."

"You sound as if you—wanted her to run away."

"Bob, there's something spooky about that thing. It isn't Nefertiti. It's—a thing. A monster."

"Now you're making her into something out of a Franken-stein movie. But, honey, it's just a cat. A cat with an artificial body, and a personality just like our cat. To all intents and purposes, it's Nefertiti. Our cat, only younger and stronger."

"It's the 'stronger' that bothers me. When she went through that window, I thought what she could do to us, if she got angry at us."

"You saw the *Today's Consumer* article. They don't attack humans, because the personality matrixes they're built on—the old cat—is submissive. They see us as alpha animals. There has never been a case of a robotic cat attacking its master, and how many of them have been sold?"

"But I notice you agreed when I suggested she sleep outside with the dog."

"Go to sleep. You need time to reestablish the bond, that's all. Nefertiti still loves us, but maybe you need a little time to learn to love her. Again."

They are quiet for a while. I feel dismal, as if I am sick all over again, only the sickness is inside my breast.

The humans do not love me. How will I survive if my slaves do not love me?

The woman makes little rustling noises, pulling the bedspread around her. "Suppose," she says, "there's a defect in our cat's chassis?"

"A defect? She acts just like Nefertiti did."

"Except stronger. She's stronger than a normal cat. The website didn't mention that, and neither did the vet."

"You think that's a defect?"

"I suppose I'm imagining things. Everything looks worse at night."

I crouch in the tree, watching the night pass. The shadows of the new moon cast leaf shapes, and I feel cold in my heart, and alone. I think of crying out, of meowling, as I did when I was a kitten. Then the slaves would come and pet me. Once when I was a kitten, I climbed up in this tree, and they got a ladder and fetched me down, and caressed my fur and said how silky and elegant I was.

But I can't, don't want to meowl.

Everything looks worse at night.

I fall nearly asleep on the tree branch, but something wakes me. The older woman next door screams, "Get out of my house, you filthy whore! You aren't my daughter anymore. You can spend the night in the street for all of me." And the sound of a slap.

The other woman says, "Please, Mama. I'm sorry. I'll get another job."

I scurry down the tree and see the door open: a little shaft of light, then darkness. But someone is sitting on the back steps of the house next door.

I steal soundlessly across the grass and slink against her thigh. She raises her head and looks at me with red, swollen eyes. My female slave had such eyes when she took me to the bad doctor that last time. "You're a pretty thing, aren't you?" she says. Her hand glides over my back fur. "What's your name? My

name is Gretchen. I wish I could have a cat. But how would I pay
for cat litter and cat food, and the vet?"

I rub against her, basking in the *PLEASURE*.

She pets me for a long time, and I see her face is more peaceful. I can read human faces; it is an art I learned from my mother.
I lean against her, and she lifts me into her lap.

"You're heavy! And you feel—I don't know, lumpy. You look
like a Siamese, but what kind of cat are you, really?"

She talks too much. Maybe the other woman won't let her
talk in the house, so she talks to me.

I curl in her lap and purr. She is not my slave, but she will do,
because she is warm and soft and babbles soothingly.

But the older woman throws open the door and light streams
out on us. "Get in here and finish ironing these sheets! My bed
isn't made, and I have to get up at eight!"

"I thought you—"

"Make up my bed first. And do the dishes. You think we
have a dishwasher, like rich people?"

"I'm sorry," says Gretchen. *I'm sorry* is her most frequent call,
like a meow. She turns again to me, reluctant to let me go. "My
mother won't let me have a cat. I'm going to have a baby, and
she says I can't have a cat and a baby both. But she wouldn't let
me have a cat before I got pregnant, either. So, I'll see you
around, pretty kitty." And she is gone.

I go back to my house and scratch on the door to my house.
Nobody answers, so I climb the tree and meow.

My slaves are in the bedroom, and they wake up. "It's her. I'll
go down and let her in."

"You sound as if you don't want to."

"What can we do? I can't let it stay out all night. It's got feelings, if we are to believe the website."

"We don't have to keep it. We could take it back, get it deactivated."

"Oh, just like we euthanized her before."

"Well, you sound as if that's what you want. What are you
thinking?"

"I think Nefertiti is really dead. This isn't her."

"So we should take it back. I can't think of asking for our money back—it would be like blood money."

She sighs. "No, we can't do that. But I can't connect with this —thing. It seems—mechanical."

"Well, sure. It is mechanical. A clockwork cat."

"I'll go down and let it in. It must suffer, in its way."

What does *euthanized* mean? Take it back? They mean me?

I run. My legs are long, strong. I can last forever. I do not need food. I am unafraid of dogs and bigger cats.

And I live in the weeds, under porches, and in flower gardens, for a long time. The days and nights come and go. It gets cold at night, and even in the daytime.

I miss my slaves. Nobody pets me, except children sometimes, and old humans who see me on the street. I sleep on empty porches in patches of sun, and I watch. I was stupid when I was sick, and before that, too. Before I became strong. I think I am what they call a robot. But I was once Nefertiti, and I have something in me that wants love. It is more than the need for *PLEASURE* of touch. I want a slave to be mine. A human.

So I go back to my house, where my slaves live. I climb the tree and look in the half-open window.

In the exact center of their bed is a small white kitten. It is licking itself. When I hiss at it, it sees me through the window and freezes, then jumps down and flees.

As I watch, my female slave comes back into the room. She has retrieved the white kitten and is stroking it. Its eyes are half-closed. It thinks it owns her.

I watch, furious and stricken, for a long time. Then I go down the tree and slink into a bush. The German Shepherd comes nosing after me, but I hiss, and it trots away.

The neighbor human I saw before, Gretchen, is huddled, shivering, on her back steps. She gets up and ambles over to me.

I see that she is fat, in the way of females who are about to drop young. "Hi, pretty kitty. I thought you belonged to the neighbors. May I pet you?" And she strokes me and strokes me and the *PLEASURE* rolls into my body like a wave of heat. I purr and rub frantically against her. "You're a stray, aren't you? Look, your fur is all full of burrs." She picks a few of them out.

"I wish you could come and live with me. But my mother would kill you. Sometimes I'm afraid that she'll kill me. Or my baby. My husband went away. He was going to be my husband. We're too young to get married. I think his parents sent him to military school."

I listen to her chatter. Her words mean very little to me, except that she is sad, and the older woman hits her. I know this, because her eye is bruised now, all purple. I saw this once when my male slave came home wounded. Another male hid in a dark place and pounced on him, then took his money. Money is very valuable to humans, and they will hurt each other for it.

"I wish you could live with me. But she'd say you cost too much to take care of." She sighs. "If her dinner isn't ready when she comes home, I'm in deep shit. Especially if she's had one for the road. So, stay out there, kitty."

She puts me down, and I mewl a tiny protest, but she is firm. She closes the screen door and looks through it at me. It's getting cold, these days, and she closes the door and goes inside.

She could keep me forever, and I'd never want anything except to be petted. My insides hurt, not with physical pain, but with a wanting and needing for the *PLEASURE* and for something else: for a slave. For love.

Gretchen didn't quite snick shut her screen door, and I pull it toward me. I'm stronger than that white kitten my slaves have brought into my house. I can open doors. Even doors to the neighbor's house, where I have never been.

The main door is harder. I think and think, and remember that humans do something with the knob. I stretch up and put my paws on either side. I press my paws together so the door knob is caught between them.

Nothing happens.

I remember: you turn it somehow.

The door unlatches with a click, then creaks open. Just a crack. Big enough for a big Siamese cat. My whiskers just brush the door and the jamb, on either side.

I scurry into the house. There are stairs. Upstairs was a good place, in my other house, the only house I know. Upstairs has closets, places to hide. I can hide for a long time.

I find a closet. If I could smell, I suppose it would smell of perfume and sweat and shoe leather. I leap to the dresser, then to the top shelf, and huddle behind a box of sweaters.

I sleep, but my mind listens.

A car grumbles up the drive, stops. The car door slams. "Why is this door standing half open?" The voice of the older woman.

The younger one, Gretchen, says something soft, appeasing.

"You think I'm drunk, don't you? You left the door open, you wasted a hundred dollars in heating oil. Pay attention! I'm your mother, not some mollycoddle teacher you can put one over on."

They argue. The girl sounds frightened. The mother is working herself up to a rage. She is a dominant animal who snaps and rages and hits and claws. The younger one, Gretchen, is too submissive. Gretchen needs lessons in scratching back.

I wait. There will be sunny, soft places to sleep in this house. There will be cat food, though I will not actually eat it. There will be petting and purring, and I will sleep on the bed with Gretchen, and she will be my slave. There will be catnip. The word *catnip* in my mind lacks the fragrance I relish, but sooner or later, Gretchen will say, "catnip," and life will be complete.

Meantime, I wait for the mother to come upstairs. If she kicks me, she will regret it.

PIGEON DROP

A CAT TOLD me this story. I was looking up relatives who I heard lived somewhere in Campobasso, and during my search I encountered this ancient feline hunting voles on the wall of the Borgo Antico in Termoli. He was walking on the wall, which was almost vertical, picking his way, very sure-footed. I believe this cat's name was Massimo, but he mentioned it only once and after would not repeat it.

He told of Puntino, a half-grown kitten, perhaps a relative of his. This little Puntino knew no magic himself, but lived with Cagliostro, the Mage of Venice, along with a pigeon named Semiramis. Puntino was entirely black except for a white diamond on his chest. His mother had been feral, and perhaps the rest of his litter remained so, but he picked scraps of meat from the cacciatore left over on Cagliostro's plate, and he purred at the magician's feet.

Cagliostro traveled the circuit and during high season never spent more than three successive nights in the same bed. The mage was ambitious, always striving to create new tricks. The pigeon Semiramis was the star of his current finale.

Puntino at first played too rough with Semiramis the pigeon, but after a while, he grew more gentle and considered the bird his friend. However, every morning, the bird would shriek in terror, until Puntino calmed her by catching her and letting her go several times. She seemed to settle down and even show guarded affection to both cat and magician during the off-season, when Cagliostro retired to a villa in Rodi Garganico.

"Why so nervous?" Puntino meowed at the bird sometimes, but Semiramis never answered. She couldn't talk, he decided, only coo in that soothing way cats like.

For one engagement, the magician's lodgings were directly above the theater where he performed, and so Puntino slipped down and draped himself on the back of an unsold seat in the balcony to watch. A pianist played bits of Puccini overtures and also Tartini's "The Devil's Trill Sonata," to build suspense for the magician's tricks, music Puntino found almost as delightful as his lost mother's purr.

At the finale, Cagliostro crowed, "And now I present my longtime avian companion, the honorable Semiramis, a dove of noble birth and intrepid spirit!" The magician always referred to Semiramis as a dove, since it sounded more elegant than "pigeon." Cagliostro invited children in the front rows to offer the bird crumbs, and Semiramis pecked at these warily.

With a flourish, the magician placed Semiramis's cage on a table at the front of the stage. He made a show of demonstrating that there was no hole in the tabletop, and nothing underneath the table. He even asked a small boy in a sailor suit to come up and crawl underneath it. The boy did so, waving shyly at his parents in the third row.

Cagliostro then clapped sharply, and a massive safe, half as big as a steamer trunk, descended from the fly space. The safe, suspended on a rope, dangled ponderously above Semiramis in her flimsy cage on the table.

The bird hopped about as if having a presentiment. Puntino's ears perked forward and his green eyes glistened with interest.

Cagliostro mounted a stepladder and drew out a sword

which he'd used in a previous trick. The pianist leaned into the ivories, rumbling forth arpeggios in a minor key.

Then the magician slashed the rope that suspended the safe. It fell! The audience gasped.

Crash! The massive safe utterly smashed the cage. The table rocked, but did not collapse. Feathers swirled in the air. Was that a spatter of blood? Exciting. Frightening.

The audience tittered and shifted in their seats, but Cagliostro descended to the stage floor with a triumphant smile. He reached into the pocket of his silk waistcoat and with a flourish produced a slip of paper. He perused the message, then twirled the dial of the safe. The minute he had opened the door, Semi-ramis, uncaged, unharmed, fluttered out.

Cagliostro nimbly caught the bird's legs. She cooed, obviously unhurt.

How had the magician done this? Puntino was only a nine-month-old kitten, but he knew that the magician's other tricks were all bogus—devices purchased by mail order or made by his own clever assistant, a dwarf girl named Lucrezia who lived near Termini.

Puntino padded back up to the magician's digs, settled on the soft rug at the foot of the bed, and thought about this.

When the show moved to a new theater, Puntino followed Cagliostro to see if perhaps he had made a deal with a minor devil. Perhaps some of the magician's magic was real.

The magician set out for the theater, only a few blocks away. As always, he wheeled his gear on a cart, with the safe strapped securely in front and the bird cage dangling from his arm. But instead of going directly to the theater, he detoured to a verdant piazza. Puntino pussyfooted after him, curious as only a green-eyed black kitten can be.

Cagliostro opened the door to the safe easily. Aha. The magician had the combination memorized, and the consultation of the slip of paper was all just for show. Then Cagliostro squatted on his heels in the grass and strewed breadcrumbs about his feet.

After a time, the pigeons pecked closer to the magician.

Cagliostro's quick hand whipped out and grabbed one by the feet. He stuffed it into the safe and snicked shut the door.

Now the magician had two doves, two Semiramises. He dusted off his hands and headed for the theater.

A ticket-taker shooed Puntino away at the door, so he hid under an awning that had blown down. He waited until two dancers in the previous act came out through the stage door to escalate some lover's spat. Then he slipped inside, like a wraith.

The pigeon act went as it had before, but this time, Puntino was sure he saw blood and possibly even, with his alert cat senses, heard a pigeon shriek.

When scraps of meat from the cacciatore appeared in a dish on the floor that night, Puntino refrained from eating them. "Not hungry, kitten?" said Cagliostro. "I'll give you a special treat if you help me create a new trick."

Puntino had no way to tell anybody the secret of his master's pigeon trick. But he tried valiantly to warn the new Semiramis. *Pietosa!* She listened, then tried to fly away, but the windows were closed and the magician let her flap around until she lay exhausted on the wooden floor. Then he put her back in her cage.

One day, Cagliostro came home with another black cat in his arms. This one was entirely black, with no white diamond on its breast. He put the cat down in front of a plate of leftover cacciatore, and it ate the meat bits avidly.

Puntino hissed a warning, but the new cat only licked its whiskers and dove into the plate to lick the sauce.

When the magician opened a bottle of ink, Puntino was gone.

So said this ancient cat, this Massimo (if that was truly his name). But how can you trust a cat of Termoli? Cats are all liars, and particularly those of the Borgo Antico of Termoli.

I did find the descendants of my great-grandfather, Guiseppi Antonio Torzillo, but my Italian was laughable, and I never got to tell them the story of Puntino. And anyway, I don't think they like magicians.

THE PAINTER AND THE SPHYNX

I AM NOT A CAT. People get that stupid idea when they look at me. I am a Sphynx. Sphynxes are special, more intelligent. Dog-like, I've heard my human's friends say. But I am not dog-like. I've seen dogs on my human's computer screen, and they are slobbering idiots.

My human, Doctor Billie Blake, forbids me to go back into the basement. However, I'm curious. I'm also perpetually cold, and the basement is warm and purring.

Doctor Billie picks me up and scolds me if I sit by the register to get warm. It will dry my skin, she says.

An animal stares at me from the big glass on top of Doctor Billie's dresser. She calls the big glass a mirror. The thing mimics me. If I lick a paw, it does likewise. It slow-blinks me with its huge green eyes. It is black, like me, and has no fur, like me. I would love to jump on it and bite its ears. Then I would settle down and lick its face, and take a nap.

It looks like a cat, but cats have silky fur and smaller ears. Their skin isn't folded in elegant wrinkles like mine.

Also, cats do not wear costumes. My human dressed me in a hoodie with wings and horns this morning. My ears stick up through holes in the hood, behind the horns. I fought her, but she says that since I am furless, I would be cold without clothes.

I know what to do about being cold. I sit on top of my human. She feels nice and warm. And then she pets me and tells me my skin feels like suede. Whatever that is.

But if she is running around and won't sit down, there is always the heat register.

The best thing is when Art comes over and they get under the covers. When they get through wrestling, I squeeze between them. It is nice and warm and we all fall asleep.

The costume my human put on me this morning is red. I'm not sure what red is, maybe a smell. She said it was for Halloween. I have not heard of Halloween before, but apparently we dress up for it. After dinner, she gets dressed up, too: a mask with ears, a striped furry suit, and a tail, to make her look like a cat.

I am not a cat.

Light fades from the sky outside. The doorbell rings. My human goes to answer it, and I see three humans. The littlest one, just a kitten, sports bright colored wings. I'm not sure if they are fake. The other small human, dressed in fur, has pointy teeth, probably fake. A bigger human hovers behind them.

My human meows at them, then gives them some rocks that small humans like.

The small girl human sees me and squeals, "Oooh, cute! What's his name?"

"Luvah," says my human.

"Why did you shave that cat?" asks the other small human.

My human laughs. "He was born that way. He's a Sphynx. They have a gene that makes them bald."

The smaller fur human (I think he is a boy human) says, "Where'd you get him?"

"From my boyfriend. A scientist. After he got his DNA, he gave him to me on Valentine's Day."

The big human squints at me. "A lab animal? He's experimental?"

"My boyfriend is researching the historical origin of the mutation that causes hairlessness. It's recessive. I won't bore you with the details."

The big human (their mother, I think) says, "Interesting! And how is your research at the U going?"

"I was fired," says my human. "They said my research might make the planet implode."

The mother's mouth drops open. "Oh. That's—too bad."

"It's all right," says Doctor Billie. "I can continue my research, and my boyfriend's, without having to account to that ignoramus dean about my ten thousand Tesla magnets."

"That's—"

"Yes, a lot of magnetic field. I discovered a method of shielding for it. I need it for my machine."

"Your machine?" She puts her hands on the heads of the two small humans, as if to protect them.

"Yes. A synthetic wormhole. So it won't plunge to the center of the Earth."

The mother human looks around nervously. Her little girl has been petting me, and she pulls the girl away.

That's the way the evening goes. Small humans pretending to be bats, or birds, or dogs, or cartoon people. My human, doling out rocks wrapped in paper, and swigging from a bottle.

They admire me, all except two who are scared of me. Not sure why.

Bored, I vault up to the top of the china cabinet and perch there, curling my tail into a perfect spiral that my human praises. I drowse.

My human rouses me by stroking the side of my jaw. "Ohhh, you feel so soft and warm!" she says, "Like an expensive glove. And you've grown. Be a good little Sphynx and come up to bed now." So I jump down onto her shoulder.

I love my human, but after she takes off her cat costume, gets in bed, and falls asleep, I pad down to the heat register in her craft room, and use my paw to pry the grating off. It's been loose for a long time, and she never fixes it.

I've always wanted to get down there again. If I try to go down using the kitchen stairs, she grabs me and hisses words like, superconducting magnets and ten thousand Teslas, and fall to the center of the Earth otherwise. There is no reason I would remember these words, except that I've lived here since I was a kitten, and although I do not speak English, I understand it well.

Then I whoosh down into the basement. I twist around to land on my paws. The landing on the hard floor jolts me. I shake my head and orient myself.

It is warm and something is softly purring.

When I was down here before, the basement was dark except for a soft color I call murr. I made that name up because my human does not have a name for it. I don't think she can see it.

But tonight, the basement is filled with light from the big round mirror floating above the magnets. I know these things are called magnets, because my human talks about them to her friend Art.

The mirror is a big ball, and there is another place inside it. I expect to see the strange animal there, just like in her bedroom mirror, but instead there is a sunny field of grass, with creatures running all over.

I would love to play with the mice, or even the bugs. If I tried to get through the mirror in her bedroom, I would just knock my head against the head of the strange animal that wears a devil costume like mine.

But when I put my paw against the surface of the mirror, it goes right through.

I feel cool wind and sunshine on my paw.

A mouse! I leap forward and pounce, but miss, and it skitters away. I chase it through the grass. It runs a zig-zag path, then disappears.

The grass is tall, and I can't see the mouse, or much of anything except grass. I freeze, then nose forward. The grass smells like the breeze when my human opens a window. Light pours down from above. I sit and look up, and the sun dazzles my eyes.

I am outside! Daytime! My human never lets me outside, but I am not afraid of the sun or the wind. I stand on my hind legs and look back at the mirror I came through. And then all around.

Bugs! Mice! Fun! I eat a green bug.

I frisk and chase. So many toys! I never ate a bug before. Now I will try a mouse.

Mice are harder to catch than I expected. I sit in the high grass, tired of the frolic.

Time to go back?

I try to retrace my path, but I've trod down too many pathways in the grass and I can't see the mirror.

I sit and wash my paws.

The skin on my ears begins to feel tender. I'm glad now that my human made me this hood that protects the top of my head. But my ears stick out and the sun pours down on them. The sun is hot, but the air is getting cold.

I lie down in the grass and purr my self-soothing purr. It is quite different from my love-human purr or my delicious-food purr. It is the purr I would make if I were sick. I have never been very sick, but if I were—

The sun slowly descends and it gets chilly, so I stand on my back paws and look for the big round mirror again. But it is nowhere. I can't get back to the basement. I can't get back to Doctor Billie.

This is the time of day when I like to run around finding things my human can't see—shadows of the murr color, motes of dust, flashes of light.

So I run around, this way—no, that! Back! Is that a mouse? I can't see over the tops of the tall grass, but suddenly I thump into a wood thing.

It's a tree.

I wish I had whiskers. I understand they help with balance and finding one's way in narrow spaces. But I have no whiskers, any more than I have fur.

I do have claws. My human keeps them trimmed, and one time she tried to paint them.

I climb the tree and begin to scream.

Maybe Doctor Billie will hear me through the big round mirror. Wherever it is.

I am miserable.

When I wake up, a smelly man in a brown woolly pair of pants and shirt is standing under the tree.

He opens his mouth and says words I don't understand, something like "oon exa daivoo!"

And then he is gone.

I am afraid, and climb higher in the tree.

He returns with a woman dressed in a brown skirt and blouse, an apron, and a white cap. The man and woman both wear shoes that look like wooden boats. She is carrying a pitcher of something that smells good. He is carrying an urn that smells like water.

He dips a thing like a bulb in the water and squirts it at me.

It reminds me of my human trying to bathe me, which I hate. So I hiss and claw my way still higher in the tree.

The man and the woman confer. Soon they are in agreement, and the woman pours some of the milk into a dish she has brought, and she puts it down on the ground.

They retreat.

I wait for a long time, and then I realize I am hungry. My human does not give me milk; it is bad for me, says her friend Doctor Wabash, the one who pretended to be so nice, then stuck a needle into me.

The milk smells so nice. Doctor Wabash is wrong. The milk is good for me, especially when I am hungry.

It isn't as easy to get down the tree as it was to get up, I have to use my brain in new ways, and make my paws work backward. But I remember my human telling me, "You're a clever little Sphynx, Luvah! Look what a mess you've made!"

I descend and pad up to the dish of milk. I thrust my tongue in and lap it up. It's so good!

—until the male human barks "Hob hem!" and grabs me by the scruff.

I struggle, raking his arm with my hind claws. I try to bite his thumb. I let out my most horrifying scream, a scream that terrifies even me.

But no. Nothing helps. He thrusts a bag over my head, over my whole body, and I can't see, I can't get loose! My meows turn to pitiful squalls. I thrash to exhaustion, lie panting and afraid, then start struggling again.

He is carrying me somewhere. A long, long walk.

At last he puts me down on a hard, rough surface. I claw out of the sack.

I am in a cage. In a room.

The two, woman and man, scrutinize me. The woman says, "ya, een daivoo."

The man human laughs and puts his finger between the bars. "Hallo, kleena daivoo!"

They keep saying that word, "daivoo." They must think this is my name. I try to say human words, though my mouth is not made for it. "Llllaah," I say plainly. But they don't care. They go off and leave me. For the night. I rumple the sack into a bed to lie and sulk upon.

I gaze around. The windows are shuttered, and very high up. Shelves carry jars and bottles and brushes. A stove squats in one corner. The evening has become cold. The stove, I hope, will heat the room.

I am still hungry, and a bit thirsty.

I need to urinate, but I am too civilized to pee in this cage. The room I am in smells awful as it is. A chemical stink like Doctor Billie's craft room, but also with unwashed bodies, something burned. I will not add to it.

Morning comes, and the woman opens the cage door and gives me a saucer of milk. The man says, "Ya, daivoos drinken melk!" I begin to catch on to some of their words. They speak something like my human speaks, English, but drawled and slurred. I will understand them if I listen.

Then I will tell them my name is not Daivoo.

I lap the milk efficiently, but not so ravenously that they think

I am too hungry.

I am replete. I lie down on the heap of rough cloth that was my sack, and I purr.

"Zolas een daivoo," says the woman.

The man and woman begin talking in an animated way, and the words "cat" and "geen" keep coming up. They must believe I am a cat. But I am a Sphynx. We are superior to cats. It is true that my ancestors were cats, but my human has assured me that they had special genes (recessive? was that the word she used?) for Sphynx kittens.

The man comes back to my cage and says "Hayz iss een daivoo. Een daivoo!" and more words that I cannot make out, but now he is brandishing a brush and I am afraid he will poke the brush into my cage and put paint on my nose.

All during their argument, my belly has been growling and cramping. I finally scamper to the corner of the cage and let loose a shameful movement.

They both jerk away from me.

The woman takes my saucer away, muttering something about "flaiss," which I hope does not mean fleas, because I am immune to fleas.

I crawl back to the sack. I circle round and round, making my bed. Then I settle with my face pointedly turned away from them. Daivoo indeed!

The old woman scrunches up her face and cleans the horrid mess up with straw and wet rags.

Thank Bast.

Later, when my belly settles, the woman sticks a morsel into the cage. "Fiss," she says. Well, that's a word I recognize, although she's saying it wrong. Fish. I nibble fastidiously. It has little needles in it, unlike the fish Doctor Billie gives me. I work around these, and leave a small portion so the smelly woman doesn't get the idea that I would grovel for her favor.

After I have eaten, she looks at me pensively and utters more words that include the word "daivoo." Again, I want to tell her I am not Daivoo, but Luvah, an important Sphynx. She opens the cage, ties a length of string around my neck, and lifts me down to the floor.

I don't like the string around my neck, but I look around to see if I can find the way to the big round mirror to go back to Doctor Billie's basement. Instead, I see the man, who has put his paint brush down.

Seeing me out of the cage, the man picks me up and takes me to a big square board propped up on some sticks, with colors on it. I see at once that it is a picture. But it is a picture with many creatures I have never seen before. He seems especially excited by the picture of a small black catlike animal with big ears, a fat belly, no fur, with red horns and wings. He babbles "daivoo" and "danky vel satan." Satan? I have heard of Satan. Back at our house, my human jokes about Satan, especially on Halloween, but Satan is also supposed to be bad. I also remember dimly that my human, my own dear Doctor Billie that I love so much, said for Halloween she was dressing me as a devil.

It all tumbles in place. The animal in the mirror in my human's bedroom. That animal is a picture of ME. I look like a devil, then?

Oh no. This scruffy little man thinks I am a devil, and he is painting a picture of me. My human would call him a painter, one who makes pictures. Pictures of me, in this case.

And he wants to keep me so he can draw more pictures of me. But I want to go back to Doctor Billie!

I have to get rid of the hoodie and cape with wings and horns that my human made for me. They don't realize it comes off, that I have many other coats, much nicer than this one.

This outfit has gotten dirty and torn. Grass and thorns stick to it, and I think maybe it got soiled when I had the accident in the corner of my cage.

The female human takes me outdoors to a patch of earth. It's colder than it was before, and it takes me a long time to figure out she wants me to urinate.

No problem. I oblige, and scratch dirt over it.

Then I make a break for the road. But no! A sharp yank on

my neck and I spin around and tumble to the dirt. I forgot about the string around my neck.

I slink back in behind her. She does, after all, give me fish. Okay, it's raw, but I'm hungry.

Also, I'm cold. Neither the woman nor her son—or husband —or master—has allowed me to bed down with them.

They don't smell good. The man smells stronger than the woman, but neither smells nice like my own human, my Doctor Billie, who has a subtle fragrance like a flower or like shampoo.

I miss my own beautiful human! I wish my mouth could form words so I could beg them to take me back to her.

In the night, I claw the neckline of my costume up to my mouth, and I chew on it. It just gets all wet and twisted, but I keep working on it. I finally give up and fall asleep.

But it is not in my nature to sleep when it is dark, unless I am cuddled up between Doctor Billie and her boyfriend. So I get up and nose the latch on the door to my cage. I know how to work doors, like the ones on the kitchen cabinet back in my home. Actually, Doctor Billie put what she calls childproof locks on them. I am not a child, but they defeat my claws. But before that, I was able to work them and I found all kinds of fascinating things inside to play with. Doctor Billie screamed when she saw I had chewed open a bag of white stuff and got it all over the floor. I guess I must have got it on myself, too, because she took me in the bathroom and gave me an especially fierce bath.

But now, I use my nose and claws and teeth on the latch. It's hard work.

By morning, I am out of the cage and on the ground. I go to work on the door to the house, but before I can do much, the man comes and pulls me away. He babbles something and straightens my coat, which I had almost got off.

He shoves me back in the cage, and latches the door again. All that work for nothing.

I look down at the ground for the source of a new scent, something impelling and delicious. But not food. And I am eye-locked with a cat. The cat has white, orange, and black fur, very stylish. The cat has not been in the room before. Maybe it was outside, hunting for those mice.

I know immediately that she is a girl cat.

She hisses at me.

I hiss back, what else can I do? She smells yummy. If I get out, should I fight her? I am a Sphynx, and she is a mere cat. I would easily overpower her.

But instead, I take a nap.

When I awake, I don't see the painter and the woman, but the cat remains in the room. She stares at me. I hiss at her again. She pads over to my cage, jumps up on the table, and bats at me through the wooden spokes. I bat back. She stands on her hind legs and pushes at the top of my cage. I emit an enraged snarl and claw at her. She lunges again and the cage falls to the floor.

The door to the cage springs open.

I am on her in a flash. She rolls on her back, trying to slash my belly. I realize belatedly that her fur protects her from my slashing paws. I have no such protection.

Her claw slices a gash in my belly, and I howl in pain and outrage.

We roll in fury, then suddenly and mutually dance away from each other. We face off, her fur erect, my every sense alert. She flattens her ears, then averts her amber gaze and backs away from me, hissing.

She retires to a corner and settles compactly, her paws and tail tucked under her body. She watches.

I think I have won this round.

Of course I have no idea if I really won, because I've never been in a fight before.

Maybe I should be more polite to her.

Without showing that I am stealing glances at her, I lick the wound on my belly.

When the man and woman come home, laden with bags that smell like cheese and sausage, he picks me up. The woman rushes up and clucks over the wound in my abdomen. But she appears also concerned with the condition of my costume, which has suffered further soiling and snags.

She rounds on the girl cat and snarls a volley of what must be curses. She picks up a broom. The cat rises to her feet, back arched, and slinks out the open door. The woman spits more curses after her.

The woman and man pet me tenderly and put me back in the cage, not noticing that the latch is broken. They give me some more raw fish, and this time I nibble more easily around the little sharp parts. But then there is a long discussion with the word *daivoo* coming up frequently. They look accusingly at me, and later let the tricolor cat back in the house.

Nobody but me realizes that the cage door no longer latches. Not even the nasty cat.

When they go away, perhaps to sleep, I paw the door to my cage open. I need to investigate many things. The door to the house, how it locks. Where they keep pieces of fish. Why the female cat smells so good.

When the man and woman wake up, I am safely back in my cage.

But the cat is eyeing me. She knows.

The next day, the woman takes me into a dark room. She lights some candles that make a smell like burning fat. She puts me on a table. I immediately jump off, and there is a struggle of will until she gives me a tidbit of some kind of dried fish which makes me lie down on the table and tear it apart with my teeth. It's not all that good, but I am hungry.

She puts some weeds in a dish and uses the candle flame to burn them. They smell sweet at first, but then they bother my nose.

She draws black lines on the table around me. I don't like this, but I am sleepy, so I don't get up.

Next, she begins to speak in a sing-songy voice. I think the words come out of a book she is holding. The language sounds different from the one she uses with the man. Sort of Halloween-sounding words. She puts the book down, then dances and pulls off her blouse and skirt. She is naked, like me, but I think not as well-formed as Doctor Billie. Too skinny.

I pull my four paws underneath my body and wrap my tail into the spiral Doctor Billie so praises. The woman continues to dance and chant.

The smoke from the burning weeds grows thick, and makes me close my eyes.

I doze.

Until her hands fall on me.

I blink open and notice she is holding a big sharp knife.

I spring out of her grip and flee to the door. It is closed, and I can't figure how to open it. I claw at the door handle and try to climb the wood. The naked woman is after me with that knife.

She lunges, but I evade her. I cower under the table. She upends it and grabs my left back leg. I shriek and claw at her. One good bite on her naked arm, and she lets go.

I scrabble behind the top of the fallen table. She kicks it aside and I flee to the other side of the room. A whole set of candles burn on another table. I leap up onto that one, not caring that my skin might be burned.

The table tips and falls over, dumping the candles. One falls on the woman's skirt and the cloth begins to smolder.

She stops chasing me and tries to extinguish the burning garment. She jerks away and sucks at her hands, which must be scorched.

I scrabble at the door, trying to work the latch. When I turn to look at her, she is squatting—planning to put the fire out by peeing on it?

The door bursts open.

It is the man. The painter.

In four swift strides he goes to the burning clothes, turns the table upside down and uses it to smother the flames.

The man picks up the knife and shakes it at her. She cries and covers her face. She holds the book to her naked breasts and wails. The two shriek at each other.

He snatches the book away from her.

The word *daivoo* is uttered a lot. Also another word, hex.

I freeze in terror. But I must run! I do not know the rooms of this house except for the one where the man paints, where my cage is, so I bolt there. Hide! I spy a high shelf where the painter keeps jars and bags and boxes. I leap up to it, barely managing to get my claws into the wood. Then I yank the rest of my body up.

The woman flees to a room I cannot see, and the man shouts after her. After a while, he comes back to the room where I am. He is carrying the book.

He opens the door to the stove and hurls the book in. Then he touches his forehead, his chest, and each shoulder. He seems to have forgotten me.

The fire flares as if the book is burning. It is gone! But he puts the knife down on the table with his paints. I am afraid he will put me back in the cage, but he kneels and clasps his hands together.

I must get out of here. This woman wants to kill me. Will the painter keep me safe?

How can I trust him?

I stay still as one of the creatures in his pictures.

After a while, I notice the calico cat is creeping along the wall under my hiding place. She sees me. She stretches, rolls luxuriantly on her back, and yowls.

Please, I think, *don't call attention to me.*

She smells delicious.

The painter is still on his knees, eyes closed, hands clutching each other. Doctor Billie and her boyfriend Art are not much into praying, but I recognize praying when I see it, from television and the computer.

After a few minutes, the painter gets up and goes back toward the room where the woman tried to kill me. He's back in a second, looking around. For me.

He doesn't see me.

I am above his line of vision, frozen. Hardly breathing.

Then the calico cat starts yowling again. It sounds like she's in pain. Is she trying to tell the painter where I am?

She continues to yowl, and every so often she lifts her tail up, then drags her rump on the floor. Something is wrong with her! Is she hurt?

The painter opens his eyes and barks at her, "How ye mount!" I can pretty well guess that means "shut up."

She does, for a minute. Then she starts up again. I would hate her, except that she smells so nice, and she's pretty, too, for a cat.

Wow! Maybe she's drawing attention to herself to keep the painter from finding me!

The painter yells things that must be curses, then something like "Stinken kat! Rot slet!" He grabs her by the scruff, opens the door and—

My chance!

I hurtle from my high perch and land on his shoulder, launch off it, and bolt through the door.

He lets out a roar and charges after me.

Disoriented. I have only been outside this house to urinate, with a string around my neck.

Now it is cold. A few snowflakes are sticking to the brick pavement. Where to go?

The calico is disappearing into the gloom, dodging fences and carts.

I gallop after her.

She goes down a cold, wet street. I lose her for a moment, but see her paw prints coming up to a wall, and—yes! I jump up and over!

She's still ahead. Not waiting for me, that's clear!

I charge on. Did the painter follow us over that wall? I hear him calling, but now it's sweet, as if he loves me.

Why does he want me? So he can draw more pictures of me? Or to kill me?

He's behind me, I can hear him calling, "Daivoo! Daivoo!"

The calico skids to a stop beside a low fence. She wriggles into a narrow hole under the barrier. I see her fluffy tail disappear.

I'm after her.

I have no whiskers, so I can't judge the size of the hole. Claw! Wriggle!

My big belly sticks! The scratch she made hurts!

I claw and squeeze and drag my body forward.

And I'm through.

She is sitting atop a stone, grooming her ears.

From Doctor Billie's Halloween decorations, I think what she's sitting on is a gravestone. But it looks all mossy and hard, not like the styrofoam ones in Doctor Billie's front yard.

I can hear the painter's voice, receding in the distance. We have lost him.

The calico looks at me and slow-blinks.

Then she begins to keen, soft and urgent.

How sweet her voice is! How lovely her eyes, a color darker than purple, that color I call murr.

She leaps from the gravestone and rolls ravishingly on the earth, her eyes seeking mine.

I move as if jerked on a leash.

I must have her!

I leap onto her back as she turns on her belly. I catch the scruff of her neck in my jaws. She squirms. I writhe. Her fur is softer than anything I have ever felt. Her nape is delicious in my mouth. Her smell, more luscious than anything I have ever known.

We are one being, all frenzy, all exhilaration.

I lose all control.

And it is over.

I slide off her.

Stand in uncertainty and delight.

She turns and snarls, slashing at my nose.

I dart away, stop and watch her.

I think: *What was that? Can I do it again?*

Just then there is howling. A pack of five hounds appears at the top of a small hillock. They alert, then swarm down on us.

The calico streaks away, and I try to follow her. But she is gone, and I don't know which way she fled.

I race away, the hounds after me. Out of the graveyard, past the church, into a cobble lane, faster, faster, hearing them bay almost at my heels.

Finally I think I have lost them.

But where is the calico? Did she go ahead of me? Would she seek refuge back at the house of the painter and that awful woman?

She is gone. No more soft fur. No more of her passionate, writhing dance. No more seductive meowing.

And I have nowhere to go. Who will feed me? The fish the painter and his woman gave me was not all that good, but at least it was food.

At least their house was warm. And kept out hounds.

Because there may be more hounds, and worse predators, out here in the dark.

I pad on endlessly, afraid to stop. Afraid to sleep.

Exhausted, I approach a thin old man in a black gown. I meow at him, begging for help. He brandishes a broom and swats me away.

As I flee, I hear again the word *daivoo*.

I am daivoo.

No! My name is Luvah, and I am a special Sphynx, and my human is called Doctor Billie Blake, and she lets me sleep between her and her boyfriend Art.

I want to go home. I run, not knowing where I'm going. I'm so cold. My footsteps slow, I am so tired.

I want the calico. I want to sleep curled next to her, and I want to have her again. But more than that, even, I want to be warm and safe. I want to stop running.

I stop running.

Here is a bush, dusted with white stuff. Snow. I creep under it, wishing for warmth. I am so cold.

I pull my paws under my body and make myself small. The Halloween costume my human made for me is wet, not warm at all.

My eyes close.

If I sleep, maybe it will be warm when morning comes. But maybe sleep is bad. I don't know why sleep is bad. I am miserable. But sleep is the worst thing.

I dream of the calico, of my jaws on her scruff, of her delicious smell, of how she swiped her claws at me—

Something prods me. A shoe made out of wood. I groan and turn from it, but hands scoop me up and pull me to a human's chest.

I know by the smell it is the painter.

The painter puts me under his cloak. He is warm. He walks, and I doze in his arms.

Will he take me back to the woman with the book and the knife?

No, he burned that book. But the woman—the knife—

He walks, carrying me.

I gain strength and struggle to get away. But his chest is warm, and I subside.

After another doze, I stick my head out of his cloak and see it is getting light now. I feel terrible. Did I sleep all night?

There is another smell: fish. He has other aromas on him, the stench of burning, the sharp nose of his paints, the stink of his woman, but also the odor of fish.

We are moving away from all the houses and even the roads now. We travel on a path of dirt, and then in a field.

And there is a tree.

I recognize the tree. It is the one the painter and his woman grabbed me from.

I feel myself lifted up. He grunts, lifting me as high as he can, and sets me on a stout limb. I lose hold of the branch and clutch with my claws. He catches me and readjusts me on my perch. Then stands and looks at me, and maybe he is sad. "Varwell, kliny daivoo!" And he walks away, swiftly.

I meow to him and try to scramble down the tree. He gave me a home. It was a bad home, with a woman who tried to kill me, but I got fish and there was a stove that kept me warm—

But it was not Doctor Billie Blake's home. My home.

After he is gone, I notice that he has left a piece of fish on the branch. I claw at it, cautiously. And nibble.

I am still so cold. But the snow has stopped, the sun has come up, and maybe they cooked the fish, because it's a little bit warm. I wolf down bits of it, struggling to avoid the little needles.

And after I have eaten some fish, I look around. The weeds all around the tree are trampled down, some from the painter, some from my own path here.

If only—

From this height, I can see it.

The big mirror-ball. The door back to my human.

I can't climb downward. I can't remember how to make my claws work that way. But I want to go home.

I jump.

And then my paws pound through the high grass.

When I get near the ball, I think, "It's not as big as I remember."

I go nearer, cautious.

I leap.

And I am in the dark. My tail is caught! The mirror-ball has closed on my tail! My beautiful tail that curls in a spiral that my human loves!

No. Just a wisp is caught. I am not, I realize, totally hairless. But I have lost that one hair on the tip of my beautiful tail.

My eyes adjust quickly. It is so warm, and the room is filled with that color that my human can't see, that I call murr.

I lie on the floor. I am home. I sleep.

But eventually, I need to go upstairs and see what my human is doing.

This is hard. I hurt all over. My paws hurt from running from the dogs, and from landing on the hard ground under that tree. Even my ears are sore.

But I need to find Doctor Billie and tell her what has happened to me.

Except I can't. I can't speak English, which is what she speaks. In fact, she talks and talks and talks. But I can't.

It seems there are more stairs than I remembered. And at the top, the door is latched. I reach up and try to turn the knob with two paws. Ugh. Not easy.

But then door flies open and I fall forward on the slippery, cold kitchen floor.

She scoops me up.

The kitchen light is on, which means it must be night. I wriggle out of her arms and pad over to my food dish.

She has put some soft, yummy smelling meat in it. Chicken, not fish. I am very tired of fish.

Another voice. Art, her boyfriend. "So you were right. Chicken is his favorite."

"I knew he'd come back. And be hungry!" she sobs. Well, yes, that's obvious. I eat more. That fish was not enough.

When I've had enough, for now, I walk away toward the living room which has the soft bed she made for me. I think she made it out of her own clothes, because it smells like her.

But she scoops me up again. I struggle, but of course she wins.

"What happened to you? You're so dirty! All oily, and your paws are filthy."

I feel myself being carried up to the upstairs bathroom. Sound of faucet turned on. Smell of hot water.

I struggle out of her arms. I do not like this water business!

But Art is standing in the doorway, blocking my escape. He scoops me up. "Poor little devil. What did you get into?"

The door slams shut and I am trapped in the bathroom with Doctor Billie and Art. She strips off her blue jeans, sweatshirt, shoes, and socks. Grabs me by the neck.

Holding me despite my struggles, she steps into the tub in her underwear. She lowers me into the water, and I am going to die now.

The water is warm. I flail and splash, but she holds me. Art hands her a bottle of special shampoo. At least I think it's special. She told me that once.

"What have you done to your Halloween costume?" She pulls it over my head and my ears hurt. "Your ears are sunburned! How did you manage that?"

I can't see Art, but he must have picked up my costume. "This is cute. You made it?"

"Yeah. I copied it from that book on Bosch and his contemporaries."

Art kneels down and kisses her. "You rule. My dissertation project inspires you, huh?"

"How could I resist?"

"But why Bosch?"

"I just thought it would be cute. The trick or treaters loved it. And it's the right time period for the mutation."

"About, I guess. If I'm right." He leaves, and I hear him trotting down the stairs.

I cease paying attention. The warm water starts feeling good as she takes a washcloth to my back, my belly, my cheeks, my head, my rump. She even runs it along my long spirally tail.

"What happened here?" A sudden pain as she washes the place the calico slashed me. It stings. "I have to put some antibiotic on that. Maybe have Doctor Wabash look at it."

Art suddenly slams back into the bathroom. "It's gone!" he yells.

She drops me, and I flail around, then try to claw my way out of the tub.

"What? What's gone?"

"Go see for yourself."

She grabs me and hands me to Art, who I like, but not as much as Doctor Billie, and runs. I hear her steps pounding down the stairs.

In a minute, she's back. "It evaporated! The wormhole evaporated!"

Art collapses onto the edge of the tub. I scrabble out of his arms and land on the slippery bathroom floor.

Art moans, "My research! I almost had the source of the mutation! I tracked it down to the Netherlands, back to the 15th century. I could almost prove it!"

Doctor Billie sinks to the floor. "Art, this is much worse than your not being able to prove a recessive mutation for cat baldness! My research into wormhole resonance!"

Art stares blindly at her, then closes his eyes and screams "Fuck!"

She mutters, "My previous wormholes collapsed within seconds. Why did this one stay open so long?"

Art rouses himself and says, "You're the physicist, Billie, but maybe they collapsed to prevent a time-travel paradox?"

She sighs and rests her chin in her hands. "Maybe. And maybe this one stayed open until something resolved some paradox. Luvah—"

I'm wet and cold. I limp toward the open bathroom door and down the hall. Downstairs. Find my nice warm nest that smells like my human.

I burrow into it and try to dry off.

Doctor Billie and Art are always talking about research and wormholes and mutations. I have no idea what any of those mean, but they must be very important. Just not important to me.

I wish I could tell them all that happened. The painter, the picture, the woman with a knife. The calico.

Maybe I am a cat.

I know I will never see the calico again.

But I wish I could tell Doctor Billie and Art about her.

CHOCOLATE KITTENS
FROM MARS

HERSCHEL'S EYES were as the color of grape-flavored rock candy, which is why I guess I spent so much time wanting to kiss him, as if I were twenty years younger. And he brought me silly, lovely gifts, imported from all over the three worlds.

Such as this: a heavy red satin box, heart-shaped, retro as all get out. It must have weighed five pounds, and unbalanced, as if there were something liquid inside. And when I snipped the darker red ribbon, there they were: three kittens curled up all soft and furry.

Why didn't I hear the purring until after I cut the ribbon? Herschel could explain it—probably they were in suspension until the scissors parted the grosgrain.

They were tiny, couldn't have been more than three weeks old. Eyes opened, though. One black, one white, one marmalade striped.

"They're too little to adopt, Herschel!" Although I love cats—always wanted to get another one since my first husband died—I was also a little annoyed that he'd taken it upon himself to give me not one, but three tiny dependents to feed, doctor, and clean up after.

"They're Mars kittens," Herschel explained. "And don't

worry about litter boxes and all. They only come out when you want to play. Other than that, they curl up in the box and sleep. For weeks, if you want."

The kittens stretched and yawned and tumbled out onto the carpet to play. The black one sniffed my ankle, the gray put tiny needle claws into the fabric of my jeans and climbed into my lap, and the white plunked itself down on the carpet and started to scream. Herschel picked it up and put it against the lapel of his claret-red leather jacket, where it immediately began batting at his hair, which he lets hang free when he's not at work.

I turned the box over. The back was printed with three panels: FORTE DARK CHOCOLATE, MILK CHOCOLATE, and BLOOD-ORANGE FUDGE.

"I thought this type of thing was illegal," I said.

He shrugged. "On Earth, sure. "

"Are these legal even on Mars?"

He smiled slyly. "Mars is a long ways away. The arm of the law is long, but it extendeth not past high Earth orbit."

"Don't they have to eat something?"

"Eat, sure, excrete, just a little, you'll never notice it, and anyway, if you leave the bathroom door open when they're awake they're trained to use a people toilet."

I wondered silently how something the size of the palm of my hand could balance itself on a full-size toilet seat, but I said nothing. I noticed a neat row of white plastic bottles with tiny nipples tacked to the bottom inside the box, in between where Milk Chocolate and Forte Dark Chocolate had been curled up. "This is the food?"

"Right. A simple syrup. They run on glucose plus a few extra nutrients. I'll bring you more when you need it."

"From Mars. What if the supply runs out?" I tried unsuccessfully to squeeze a drop of it out, then sniffed the nipple. It didn't smell like milk.

He shifted the white kitten to his other shoulder and reached over to kiss me. "Trust me, Ivy. The supply will not run out."

We sank back on the couch and petted each other like cats.

The kittens jumped all over us, climbing up and tickling my ear with their whiskery little snouts and padding all over our hips and backs. After a while, Herschel drew away and stroked my hair. "Say you like them, Ivy. You do, don't you?"

"How can I resist? But I worry about caring for them."

"You don't fully appreciate Martian technology. Try this." And he scooped up the black kitten and licked its belly.

"Herschel! That's disgusting!"

His violet eyes grew wide with pretended offense. "Try it, really."

"Herschel, I can't be licking a cat!"

He leaned over and kissed me again, and there was a taste on his tongue, very intense, of strong, rich dark chocolate.

I drew away. "Wow! That's from the kitten?"

He smiled his "gotcha" smile.

Hesitantly, I slid my hand under the tiny warm belly of the orange striped one. I held it to my face, and it stared at me with green, calm, alien eyes and purred.

I put my tongue hesitantly on the place between its ears where striped cats have that M marking.

Oh boy. My mouth was flooded with the richest, most expensive orangey chocolate taste I could imagine. I almost dropped the kitten.

The kitten seemed as pleased as I, and twisted its body around to tongue-rasp my thumb.

"Herschel, this isn't humane. I mean, these are real kittens. They're bioengineered, I'm sure, but somewhere back in their ancestry is a real cat, and—"

He kissed me again, that complex sweetness fading with the second kiss, and smiled his sardonic, teasing smile. "Ivy, they are in no pain. Look." He put the black kitten down and it frisked around his Nikes, then discovered its short little tail and chased it.

"But they could spend their entire lives in a little box. That's not right, Herschel."

The black kitten—I decided to call it Bittersweet, which is the moment at which I knew I was going to keep him at least—caught its own tail, bit it, squeaked, and began licking it frantically.

The orange striped one was more laid-back. It seemed pleased with the idea that I had licked it, and probably decided if I wasn't actually its mother, I was a good substitute. I put it on my lap, where it kneaded fervently, purring ever more loudly, its eyes half-closed in a sort of Buddha state. Marmalade, I decided to call it.

Why was I naming these kittens? Had they hypnotized me? I resolved not to name the white one, even though its name was obviously Ice Cream. Cream for short.

"They're no trouble," said Herschel. "And all fun. Honest." The white one was clawing at my sofa.

I always felt sorry when my friends talked about their boyfriends, middle-aged paunchy men with hound-dog eyes and shiny scalps. Herschel is forty-one, just as old as any of their boring lovers, but he's exciting. He has shoulder-length black hair, eyes the color of candied violets, and a long, hawkish face finished by a mobile mouth capable of wryness, tenderness, derision—and those kisses.

Even without the chocolate, those kisses—!

"I'll bring you more of the milk," he promised.

The kittens frisked around us as he kissed and kissed and kissed me. My last thought, before my attention turned entirely to Herschel's hands, mouth, and hips, was that Marmalade was trying to nest in my hair.

I had met Herschel online while my employer was scoping out a facility on Mars. Like many entrepreneurs, my boss felt hampered by international laws restricting biological research. Mars corporations lease habitats suited for scientific R&D. Herschel was an agent for one of these corporations.

We hooked up because of a hematite ring he mentioned

buying when we were connected, on business one afternoon. Mars hematite. He gave me a URL which carried Mars jewelry. I hadn't ordered any of it—its satiny blue gleam is best appreciated with the naked eye, not in pictures—but they told me when you scratched it, it showed a blood-red streak.

Herschel had been to Mars three times. It wasn't hard to bring back experimental products; most weren't actually illegal on Earth, just the aberrant stem cells and other research that spawned them.

He could have made a wad of money selling psychoactives too new to be against US law. But he didn't. He only brought back the occasional novelty, only for private use. Gifts for his mother, sister, nieces. And, since we had met online a few months ago, for me.

When Herschel and I came up for air, some forty minutes later, the kittens were all in their box, nursing fervently on the nipples of the white vials.

Herschel was as good as his word, and brought me a case of the kitten-milk, MicroMilk™. He said he'd give me the address of the Earth-side company that sold it—it apparently was used for something else, he forgot what—so I wouldn't have to worry about the poor little guys starving.

Herschel was as good to me as those boring men my two office mates were dating. I'd had a long run with the VR personals, and I knew what was out there. How could I be so lucky? My first husband, who died of Fell's syndrome, was a gem, but, kind and supportive though he was, not as sexy as Herschel.

How could any man top his gift?

We were going to a performance chef affair that Saturday. He said I should dress up, so I wore the little dark red number. It was cut modestly in the front, but the back showed everything down to the rouged tops of my buttocks.

I usually put the kittens back in their box when I was out of the apartment. My lease said no pets, but they were quiet, and although I was afraid they'd give away their presence by sunning themselves in the front window, they seemed to enjoy basking in shadows.

The others went willingly, but this time Cream hid under my couch. I put my hand in to pull her out, and she scratched me.

The little rascals had claws, all right. I tried to stanch the bleeding with a tissue, but it was deeper than I'd thought. Cream ran away; I knew most of her hiding places, I could get her later.

Worried about the time, I threw the dress on and was a little annoyed to find a snag in the hem of the dark red dress. Which kitten had done this? Somehow I suspected Cream, but I figured it hardly showed.

The chef was a riot, especially the knife juggling salad prep and the entrée where he produced ingredients from his hat. As a finale, he used contained explosives to finish our *bombe chocolat*.

Herschel waited until the pyrotechnics were over to tell me, over the undramatic coffee, that he had another business trip to Mars. He'd be gone almost a year. He said he understood if I wouldn't wait, but if I would—

The ring was a huge ruby surrounded by faceted hematites.

A cynic once told me engagement rings are soft prostitution; how many women have agreed to marry a man because they were temporarily hypnotized by the refractive depths of a gem?

No. This was only the icing on the cake.

I loved Herschel; it wasn't just that he was handsome and a spectacular lover; he really was good to me in many ways, the compliments and gifts, listening to my thoughts and problems.

We could write back and forth every day, Herschel said. And I'd have the kittens to keep me company. Chocolate company.

I wondered softly whether these absences might be a challenge when or if we were married, but Herschel offered to get me a position in his company. We'd travel together.

His flight to Kennedy left the next morning. So little time for goodbye kisses. I almost forgot to ask him where to get the milk for the kittens. He scribbled a URL for MicroMilk™ on the back of an envelope, kissed me again with the last of those kisses that left me weak and dizzy. And he was gone.

I let the kittens out of their box. Forget my melancholy with their antics. Bittersweet had a thing for the tip of his tail, but he could also go for Marmalade's tail. He was my pounce-pro; his genome must have included a good mouser.

When they clawed their way into my lap, I licked each one, laughing at the absurdity of it. But then closed my eyes and savored the flavors.

Belatedly, I realized I didn't even have a good photo of Herschel. I was late to work trying to capture an image of him from our many internet conversations. Unsuccessfully. Herschel's good looks didn't translate to archive mediums.

The kittens, and their chocolate flavors, were a distraction, as we continued our relationship long distance. Herschel's company let him have unlimited access to his account while he was on the Mars-bound spacecraft, but the intervals—because the craft was receding from Earth—got longer and longer between my affectionate outpourings and his erotic responses.

The kittens, all three, climbed into my lap every time I sat at the computer. Bittersweet was fascinated by my hand on the fingerpad, convinced that my pinkie was a mouse. Cream used the time to climb up my neck and, if I let her, to the top of my head, where she would curl up in my hair and try to sleep, tightening her tiny claws if I moved too much.

Absently, I'd lick them whenever I could. Great, all the chocolate I wanted, no calories, three flavors.

When Herschel and I were tired of teasing each other and playing mutual admiration games, we talked about the news (two religious groups were at war on the moon, Congress was debating a ban on brain implants in infants, the President was off his Prozac), but our most frequent conversations were plans for our future, joy and yearning. And, of course, the kittens.

I was busy the week after Herschel left, so I didn't get around to ordering the nutrient fluid for them. Then the company sent me two months' supply, again in sealed bottles. How did the kittens survive on such tiny amounts of this "milk"? I was tempted to break open one of the white nursing bottles, but the stuff was expensive, and the directions indicated that it was sterile, would be ruined by contact with air.

I no longer kept the kittens in their box; they romped or slept all over the apartment full time, even when I was at work or asleep. Their tiny warm bodies next to my head on the pillow seemed a consolation for the absence of my love, even Herschel's messages. Cream, particularly, enjoyed nestling at my throat, purring and kneading.

Herschel's craft would be cycling behind the sun in a few days, and in anticipation, he had composed a series of ten love notes, one to be opened each day.

That was when I tried to order more milk for the kittens, and discovered the company responded neither to phone calls or emails. The MicroMilk™ website had vanished, nothing but a black box with a red edge left at the URL.

I crammed them back in the box, determined not to let them use their energy until I could find something to replenish them. *"Herschel, is there an alternative source for the MicroMilk™?"* I expected it would be the first thing Herschel would read—and respond to—when the craft came from behind the sun and we could email back and forth again.

But as I lay sleepless one night (I blamed my insomnia on lack of both kittens and Herschel), I obsessed that perhaps the kittens were already dead. I got up and, without turning on a light, opened the box.

They were awake, quiescent. They gazed up at me, green eyes all. Then a car passed on the street outside, and the eyes reflected it with feral opalescence. Reassured, I tried to clap the lid back on the box, but Bittersweet had uncurled, stretched, risen, and clambered half outside. I shoved him back in, but Cream got out, then Marmalade, and it was like—well, like herding cats. They hadn't been out in three days, and they were ready to play.

They frisked around the room, chasing each other, inserting tiny claws into the cloth of my bathrobe, jumping from chair to table to refrigerator top. I couldn't keep track of them. Finally, they gathered at my feet and yowled. Yowled!

Nervously, I tried to gather them up before a neighbor complained. But they were having none of it. They were hungry.

What could I do? I offered them the empty vials, hoping the small residue or even the flavor might keep them busy, but only Cream tried to nurse on them. The other two just sniffed and began to rake against my legs, screaming in their tiny, piercing voices.

I scooped them all up, hoping that my warmth would quiet them, and went to my computer.

"Herschel, I know you won't get this for almost a week, but I really need a solution to this kitten-feeding problem. The little guys won't go back into their box. The poor little babies are so hungry!"

I opened the refrigerator (Bittersweet had always taken serious interest in it, so maybe there was something inside he might like), and my eyes lit on the coffee cream.

I poured some in a saucer, and the kittens all approached and sniffed it. Bittersweet even lapped up a drop or two. But all of them backed away hissing, then meowed even louder.

I scooped them up and again tried to put them back in the box—actually got Bittersweet inside and slammed the lid down—but the other two ran away. I gave up and left Bittersweet in the box. I could hear his muffled screams, but I hoped in a few minutes he'd shut up and go to sleep.

The other two had disappeared under a sculpture of antique AOL disks my niece had made for me. I tried to retrieve them, but got only a six-inch-long scratch for my pains. I gave up and tried to go back to sleep. After a while, I felt the tiny weight of kittens spring up on the bed with me. My last memory before going to sleep was of fur under my chin and at the nape of my neck.

I awoke groggy and weak. No answer from Herschel, of course. I tried a web search but got some ominous pop-ups that suggested I was trying to break the law. And in fact, maybe I was. The kittens were forbidden technology on Earth.

Maybe even on Mars.

The kittens stayed out of their box. I tried at one point, when I thought they were exhausted from chasing each other around my desk, to shove Cream and Marmalade back in the box, but of course this only meant that Bittersweet got out too. Now I had three starving cats running loose. I was afraid even to lick them for their flavor. Perhaps production of the chocolate alkaloids and complex flavonoids taxed their metabolism.

Every morning, exhausted and heartsick, I got up expecting to see their starved tiny bodies dead in the bed beside me, but the fact was, they were growing.

Wait a minute. Did this mean something in the box was a growth inhibitor? Bittersweet, who had spent an extra night in the box, did seem fractionally tinier than the other two—

At last, the tenth day, the spaceliner emerged from behind the sun, and Herschel's warm pixels bloomed on my screen. *"Feed them cow blood,"* was all he said.

Cow blood? You think cow blood is an easy commodity to acquire? I tried the butcher at a Tiptops three blocks from my apartment, but he looked at me strangely and I decided not to go back there ever again, even for coffee cream.

I was exhausted. I was losing weight. I looked like hell. The kittens were angry and playful and pleading by turns. Cream would dance up to me, scratch me furiously, and then, contrite, lick my hand with her tiny, abrasive tongue, cleaning the very scratch she'd made.

I tried repeatedly to trace the company that had made the original kitten fluid. I even tried eBay. My eBay search got a call from a detective. I told him I needed to contact MicroMilk™.

"You and a lot of other people," said the detective. "Including the law."

Later, I wished I'd asked him to elaborate.

"Herschel," I wrote, desperate, *"they're dying. They haven't had any nourishment in over two weeks."* But a message came back from the triplanet server: the craft was now having communications problems.

I'd have to wait until Herschel got to Mars.

I found a source for chicken blood (don't ask) but they simply looked at the saucer of the nasty stuff and then gazed at me with green-eyed puzzlement, as if I'd offered them a dish of red poster paint.

But the kittens weren't dying. They seemed quite happy, in fact.

They were, in fact, thriving. Growing. They weren't supposed to grow.

And I was beginning to get suspicious. I'd always had to watch my weight, but now my clothes were hanging on me. I tried eating real chocolate, candy, croissants, cookies, even Count Chocula with chocolate milk and Dove liqueur. None of it tasted as good as the kittens. I found myself wishing for a taste of their fur even while I was at the office. I considered smuggling Bittersweet, the smallest, into work in my messenger bag.

I wondered now if they thrived on being licked, and if the chocolate flavor was somehow destroying my health.

I tumbled to what the kittens were doing when one of my coworkers asked me why I had scratches and cuts all up and down my arms. And on my neck.

I didn't need to go to my internist to know I was anemic.

Chocolate vampire kittens from Mars.

They were cute. I couldn't put them out in the cold. Even if I wanted to: somebody else would find them, adopt them, get sucked dry by them.

And perhaps that person would be victimized without even the joy of knowing their chocolate secret.

They were way too big for the box now.

Could I have them killed?

No! It wasn't their fault that they were engineered this way. They hadn't signed up in the womb—or test tube—to be chocolate or to be vampires. They were so cute, playing around my legs, purring against my neck as I fell asleep, kneading my throat to get the blood to flow—

And the chocolate. So much better than mundane chocolate, which tasted bland and chalky, ruined by off flavors and wax and the stuff used to extend and harden it. The kittens' chocolate flavor had the slight bite of bitterness, the teasing sweetness, the richness that floods your mouth, and so much more.

Some nights I completely lost control and licked them all over, from their whiskers to their twitchy tails. The fur back of their ears was particularly delicious.

I've heard people say that chocolate is better than sex. They're wrong. But my kittens, unlike Earthly chocolate, really were better than sex.

And if I could only get some MicroMilk™, they'd be fine again.

I hoped.

Of course, they'd never fit back in their little heart-shaped coffin again.

I was hooked on the kittens, that was the problem. I no longer had the strength of will to control them, or figure out a solution to my dilemma. Once, when the scale had hit a new low and I was trying to build myself up with iron pills and milkshakes, I thought of eating garlic. Since these weren't supernatural kittens, I doubted that the old vampire remedy would help, but I did know that babies didn't like the taste of garlic in their mother's milk.

The kittens didn't like it, either. They sulked. They hid in a dark closet for days. When they came out, they tasted of garlic. Garlic and chocolate don't taste good together.

The garlic was worse than useless. They cried until my neighbor downstairs called the office, but they continued avidly to suck my blood, though complaining constantly and refusing to be petted. And then I discovered they were roaming.

I wouldn't have known what was going on, except that the upstairs neighbor mentioned that she was gravely worried about their baby. It seemed to be anemic and tests gave the pediatrician no clues to diagnosis.

I sat with Bittersweet in my lap, licking his ears and reading the news online for rumors of mysterious illness, or even *Midnight Nova* articles about twenty-first century vampire attacks.

Herschel had landed on Mars by this time. But I hadn't heard from him. I looked at the ruby ring on my finger. Hematites around the central ruby. That red streak—didn't hematites have something to do with blood?

Then I thought, maybe Herschel is—I don't know—infected. The kittens seemed to be addictive. Had he licked one? Even if he hadn't licked Bittersweet, Cream, or Marmalade, maybe he might go back to the factory and try one there.

But he had licked Bittersweet. I remembered that one bittersweet kiss.

Frantic, I emailed him, a long letter with the complete story. I was afraid his employer would read it and he'd get fired or even arrested, but he had to know the danger he was in.

His response was only, *"Don't worry, my little Earthpussy. The cats are harmless and it's hard to kill one, starvation or no."*

Hard to kill. Why didn't I like the sound of that?

His letters became curt. He didn't acknowledge my pleas for help with the cats. I asked him for the name of the company that had engineered them, but he simply rambled on and on in his next missive about a new polymetallic sulfide site his company was prospecting. They'd gone into mining, it seemed. Since Herschel was a biology specialist, he was considering switching employers.

What did this mean for me? What did it mean for my prospects of getting information to save the kittens? Or myself?

They were getting big. The male, Marmalade, showed a healthy interest in jumping the other two. What would happen when Bittersweet and Cream went into heat?

Nonsense, I told myself. Who in the world would engineer a novelty organism, a toy, to reproduce? It would ruin business.

But maybe the box was supposed to keep them prepubescent as well as tiny. Or maybe they were a beta version, organisms that weren't meant for sale.

For the hundredth time I examined the box in which they had arrived, the vials which had contained their nutrient fluid. There were no clues. Just a table showing calorie count (zero), sugar (zero), other nutrients (zero, zero, zero). FORTE DARK CHOCO-LATE, MILK CHOCOLATE, and BLOOD-ORANGE FUDGE.

I was almost too sick to go to work. My face was the color of chewing gum on the bottom of a 42nd Street theater seat. My chest rattled as if it were a box full of dried popcorn kernels. I moved through my day as if wading through a saucepan of congealing taffy.

And I was worried about Herschel. He seemed oblivious to the danger he was in. How could I get his attention, so many million miles away? I asked if he were feeling as enervated as I, and he answered finally, saying, *"Well, Mars, you know, the diet, the gravity, the dust in the air, of course he wasn't what he was on Earth, but he was okay, nothing was wrong, stop worrying, my chocolate mouse, my bird of paradise, my honey goldfish of love."*

I wanted to hit him. I wanted to scream. I considered breaking the engagement, just to get his attention so he'd take care of himself, but that would be too cruel, especially if he really were sick.

He sometimes seemed distant, as if his passion for life were gone. If he was affected by the kittens as I had been—but that was silly, he wasn't sleeping with them nightly. He wasn't losing blood to nourish them.

Still, the effects might come from mere contact. And I couldn't be sure he wasn't going to the factory where they were made, being exposed daily to their rapacious little tongues and teeth.

They were so damn cute!

And the chocolate was good. It was the only thing I really had to look forward to. Even Herschel's return, the date marked in red on my calendar, didn't thrill me as it once did. I was too sick. I worried that I would disappoint him as a lover, lying limp and unable to respond to his skilled passion.

I had searched the net for some information about the kittens themselves. I tried the names on the bottom of the box, with and without the word MicroMilk™.

I even broke open one of the empty vials.

The drop of fluid inside was viscous and dark red, and smelled—why was I unsurprised—like old blood.

But it must have something else in it. I took it to a lab, but was met by refusal. They had a policy not to work on Martian organics; the risk was too great.

I had somehow forgotten what Herschel even looked like. How could that be? The restricted bandwidth of his recent communications had prevented him sending a recent photo, and my attempts earlier had met with disappointment.

I searched his name on the net.

Herschel B. Taylor.

I hadn't expected to find so many hits. I can't remember why I hadn't done this before—or maybe I could. He'd admonished me against it, "Oh, I'm not very photogenic," and never given a reason, but those grape-candy eyes, that magnetic glance—"Oh, don't do that, I hate having my picture taken."

And in fact, there were no good photos of him anywhere on the net. He seemed—invisible.

Oh, yes, there were dozens, maybe almost a hundred hits, mostly pertaining to Mars corporations. But they were always of his back, or of his shadow, or of somebody entirely different who seemed to be sitting opposite him at a conference table, a desk, or a resort restaurant buffet.

To this day, I don't know how he managed to avoid being imaged, but I know he must have had a reason.

One image struck me with electrifying force. Herschel (that must be him, his long hair, his hand with the hematite ring holding her hand, even his burgundy leather jacket) was kissing a woman whose face was partially visible. The woman was identified as Clarice Etta Armand.

Quickly I searched her name, and a hundred hits came up, the first with a banner over her head.

CHOCOLATE VAMPIRE KITTENS FROM MARS.

She was smiling. A man unidentified in the caption (in that burgundy leather jacket, wearing that hematite ring) was kneeling in front of her, back to the camera, holding up two tiny kittens.

In another image, she was wearing the burgundy leather jacket loosely around her shoulders, and an unidentified—but oh so recognizable—man had buried his face in the hollow of her neck.

It had been taken at a Martian resort popular with honeymooners.

Clarice and the man dancing. Clarice waving as the man, his face in shadow, held her jacket.

Clarice in a space suit, out in the open on Mars, holding hands with an unidentified man in a space suit. Prospecting a new site.

Herschel's boss was a man.

"Herschel, I wrote. Silly me. Are you involved with a woman named Clarice?"

He didn't answer.

Which left me with the chocolate vampire kittens from Mars. They were clearly beta products, not meant for export. I wondered how Herschel had gotten entangled in my life. I wondered if Clarice knew about me. Wives on both worlds. Clarice a brilliant entrepreneur, me—what—a test subject?

Maybe she did know about me. Maybe they tested the kittens on me.

Which, as I say, left me with the kittens.

I locked them in my closet and lay down on the bed to think. They screamed and screamed, and I finally dressed and left the apartment. I went to work and didn't come home. Spent two nights on the floor of my office.

When I returned two days later, they were silent. I cringed, thinking them dead. But perhaps they needed to die. Perhaps it would be the most merciful thing. They had gone after that baby, after all—

But they weren't deliberate killers. And their predations were programmed into them. How could I think of them as guilty? It was Herschel who was guilty; he knew what they were. Did even Clarice, who had no doubt developed them, know what they were?

I took off my coat and listened at the closet door. They were silent, but after a moment, a small black paw slid under from the door, patted, explored, withdrew.

I waited. When it poked out again, I yearned to press my face to the crack in the door and lick that little paw.

Resisting was the hardest thing I've ever done.

After a while, I put my coat back on and went onto the street. At the Tiptops, where the butcher had looked at me so oddly when I'd requested cattle blood, I purchased three pounds of 95 percent chocolate. Back at my apartment, I broke open the packages, ignoring the bitter perfume of the stuff, and slid square after square under the door.

Kill? Or cure?

The elegant paw did not emerge again. I heard soft purring.

I'm afraid to open the door.

SCOUT

SPRING EQUINOX. *Whirring sound. Flashing lights. Whoosh of advanced propulsion system.*

"Mao! Mao! Mao! Mao! Mao! Mao! Mao!"

Door opens. "Scat! Get away from here! Go home!"

"Mao!"

Fifteen minutes elapse.

"Mao! Mao! Mao! Mao! Mao! Mao! Mao! Mao-ao-ao-ao!"

"I *told* you, scat! Nothing for you here! *Go home*!"

"Mao! Mao!"

"Go chase some mice. Or birds. I hate birds."

"Maomaomaomao-ao-ao-ao!"

Splash. "There! Does *that* convince you? Now if I can just get back to sleep."

Six hours elapse.

"What? You still here? Somebody dropped you, right? Threw you out of a car? Do you have a collar?"

"Yooooow! Sssssss! Raaaaawooo!"

"Ow! Forget it. Just be gone when I get home from work."

"Prrt."

Nine hours elapse. Car pulls up, door slams. Footsteps.

"Gone. Thank God. I was scared somebody took me for the cat lady over on Prospect."

Six hours elapse. Door opens.

"Mao?"

"Go away! I'm calling the Animal Warden and that's it. Hear me? Smoked kitty. Nice cyanide gas. Get! Scat!"

"Mao?"

"What are you doing? That has maggots on it. You can't eat that!"

"Prrrrr."

"You're eating maggoty ham, and purring? That's disgusting!"

"Prrrrrrrrrr."

"How could anything get hungry enough to eat rotten meat? Wait a minute."

Door closes, opens again.

"Here, here's the rest of my chicken wings. Hope you like garlic honey sauce. They're cold, anyway."

"Purrrrrrrrrrrrrrrrrr."

"Get away from my legs! I hate that. Didn't I tell you I hate cats?"

Door slams. Eight hours elapse.

"Thank God it's gone. Found some other sucker."

Car door slams. Car starts, zooms away.

Three days elapse.

"Mao, mao, mao, mao, mao, mao, mao."

"You again? I don't have any more chicken wings. And I

don't believe you if you say you're lost, because you left here Friday and then came back."

"Prrt?"

"Let me look at your collar. I bet some nice little stupid girl is just weeping her eyes out over you. Woosy woosy woosy woosy."

A brief chase.

"MAO!"

"Okay, so you have a collar, but no name on it. Real stupid little girl. She deserves to lose a prize fleabag like you."

"Prrt."

"At least you didn't scratch me again."

Six hours elapse. Dusk gives way to nightfall. The air chills.

"Mao? Mao? Mao? Mao? Mao? Mao? MAO? MAO? MAOMAOMAOMAO?"

A window opens.

"Shut up down there! Remember what I did the last time you woke me up?"

Footsteps on stairs. Door opens.

"MAOMAOMAOMAOMAOMAOMAOMAO!"

"Let me guess. You're cold, right? If I give you something to sleep on, you'll get cat hair all over it. And fleas. And worms. I bet you have worms, eating garbage like that."

Door closes. Footsteps, sounds of rummaging. A piece of torn, dirty carpeting falls out of an upper window, THUMBS on the ground, raises billows of dust.

"*Mao!*"

Silence.

Seven hours elapse.

Door opens. "Where are you? Did you spend the night under the rug? Great, now what do I do with this piece of shit? I

suppose I have to leave it, in case it's cold again tonight. A deco-
rator touch for my entry."

Car door opens, closes, car speeds away.

Nine hours elapse.

"Here. For Your Majesty. It was cheap, and it looks better
than that rug."

"Mao. Prrt."

"That's right. Show some gratitude, you little rat. You look
like a rat, did you know that? You aren't much bigger than a rat.
Well, hey, that's what eating maggoty garbage does for you. Not
exactly the breakfast of champions. I suppose if I give you a little
milk you'll think you can move in here, right? So I won't."

"Mao?"

"Not a chance. Go find your supper somewhere else."

"Mao? Mao?"

"And stop rubbing cat hair all over my pants!"

Door closes. Fifteen minutes elapse.

"Here! Will that shut you up?"

"Prrrrrrrrrrr. Slup. Slup. Slup. Prrrrrr. Slup slup slup slup
slup slup slup."

"That's the last you get out of me. I probably don't have
enough left for my cereal in the *morning.*"

Twenty-four hours elapse.

"Okay, one more time. But I looked up the Animal Shelter on
the web. It says they let you stay five days, and then it's curtains
for kitty cat. Okay? So I think you should move on."

Four hours elapse.

"Mao! Mao! Mao! Mao!"

"Look, I don't have any more chicken wings. How about
some—french toast? Look, it's good, it's only been in the garbage

since yesterday. Eat it. Eat it, you fleabag! It was good enough for me. Are you saying it's not good enough for you? Here, I'll butter it for you. Oh, you like that. Lick the butter off, huh?"

"Mao."

"No! I will not put more butter on it! Eat the whole thing, bread and all."

Twenty-four hours elapse.

"Mao! Mao! Mao! Mao!"

"Why are you still crying? Didn't you want the french toast? Yich! It's got flies on it."

"Waka."

"Waka? What does that mean? Cats don't say 'waka.' I'm not going to feed you if you don't speak proper English."

"Prrt."

"Wait a minute."

Car door slams. Car takes off.

Twenty minutes elapse. Car pulls up. Car door slams.

"Okay, you win. Cat food. This is probably a big mistake, but I'm not going out and buying you chicken wings."

Twelve hours elapse.

"Mao! Mao! Mao! Mao!"

Footsteps stumble down stairs. Door opens.

"At 3:00 AM you think I'm going to feed you? Oh. Your water overturned on the cat bed. Shit. Here. Here's an old sweatshirt."

"Prrt."

Four hours elapse.

"Here. You didn't ask for it, but I suppose you will. Here's your damn cat food. It stinks. I hope you love it."

"Mao."

"Is that your name, cat? Mao? Like Mao Tse Tongue? You don't look Chinese to me." (*Subject skritches cat behind ears.*) "You look—hungry. You're kind of silky—"

A succession of days in which cat food appears in margarine tub. Spring advances. Warm weather. Cat eats food. Subject puts out more cat food.

"Pretty eyes. You might clean up nice. I'd let you in the house, but you'd bring in fleas. Let me think about this."

Subject switches to more expensive brand of cat food.

"You don't want to come in? *Last chance.*"

Autumnal equinox. Whirring sound. Flashing lights. Whoosh of advanced propulsion system.

"Hey, cat! Cat! You didn't eat your food. I'm not going to buy any more unless you eat this. Hey, cat! Hey, Mao! Sneaky-paws! Where are you?"

Door left hopefully ajar.

Twelve hours elapse.

"Where are you? Pretty kitty! Mao!"

Another twelve hours.

"Where the hell are you? Mao! Mao! Maaa-oo! Mao! Mao! Mao! Mao!"

LIN JEE

THE MORNING after our wedding night, Lin Jee woke us yowling over a sock she had killed.

Almost immediately, Eric, Tom's best man, appeared in the door. "Somebody's broken in!"

Our wedding had been pretty modest, family and a handful of friends, and we stayed in the old farmhouse the next night, before departing on our honeymoon.

Lin Jee hadn't killed a sock in a long time. She used to kill mice and (what can I say?) the occasional blue jay. Like the farmhouse, she was part of the "dowry" my Granny had left me in her will. As a kitten, Lin Jee had once gone after a rat bigger than she was. I suspect she'd have killed it, if Granny hadn't snatched her up.

But Granny had passed away ten years ago, Lin Jee's fur had turned cinnamon-dark with age, and the old Siamese curled like a fur croissant in a nest near the furnace, and hunted nothing, not even socks.

And I had just married the most wonderful architect in Burton, Ohio.

That same architect, Tom, was standing in his boxer shorts in the middle of our bedroom holding a gray sock. When Eric appeared, Tom tossed the sock to me, and it landed, soggy and cold, in the middle of my chest.

Eric's eyes were wild. "That cat woke me up. God, what a voice."

My little brother Bobcat, who had apparently slept in his clothes, appeared in the doorway behind Eric. "What's up, Sis?" I looked for signs of drug abuse, although Bobcat had been in a twelve-step program for two years now, since a spectacular car crash on his nineteenth birthday.

Lin Jee ambled over to the bed, scrambled up, and presented her creamy belly for petting.

Tom pulled on his jeans, his only change of clothes since he'd flown in from the base in Hawaii for the wedding, the rest of his gear being at his folks' house until he moved in. I grabbed a long tee shirt, and we all rushed downstairs.

"The back door was standing open," Eric said. "I thought it was just Bobcat, sneaking a cigarette. Then I saw all the gifts gone."

I rushed into the parlor, still clutching Lin Jee, who purred her satisfaction at having played watch cat.

Martha, my oldest friend and matron of honor, floundered out of the front downstairs bedroom. Great with child, she probably was the only person who didn't have a hangover. Her husband, Charlie, was a cool guy, but he had a weakness for beer. He followed her out and headed for the john.

Eric ran to the back bedroom, where he had slept alone.

It was all too true. My mother had polished up Granny's sterling and put it gleaming into its velvet-lined case. But the case was no longer displayed on the coffee table in the living room. Nor were the food processor, the silver candlesticks, the linens, the crystal vase, the expensive espresso-maker, the internet-enabled flat-screen TV my parents had given us.

And the envelopes in which money gifts were enclosed were gone. But then I remembered Tom had hidden the checks and cash in the Blue Willow vase in the china cabinet.

I ran to the china cabinet, only to discover the vase gone.

Eric came back from the bedroom. "My Rolex is gone! How could I have slept through that? What the hell did you guys put in the punch?"

Bobcat stumbled to the door and looked at it. "There's some scrape marks around the latch. They must have broke in."

"I think that's from where I forced the lock last summer," I said. "I locked myself out, and I didn't want to call Mom or Dad to drive all the way over from Champion."

"You're insured, aren't you?" Charlie asked, reappearing and zipping his pants. "Has anyone called the cops?"

"I'll do it," said Eric. "You guys catalog what's missing."

Shaking, I went into the bedroom where Martha and Charlie had been sleeping, to my bill-paying desk. As I was rummaging for paper and pen, Martha took my arm. "This worries me, Mary. Charlie is just pretending to be hung over. He didn't drink any more than I did."

I looked at her, amazed. "You're saying—?"

"He's been worried about bills."

"But he just got a great new job at the bank, and—"

"Listen to me, girlfriend. The insurance doesn't kick in for six months. And the baby—"

"Is due in a month. But he wouldn't—?"

She hunched her shoulders and looked at me wide-eyed. "He asked if you had insurance."

Sure, we had insurance. But it didn't cover antiques, like the silver.

From the front bedroom, I could see out into the yard. The brilliant sun made the grass sparkle with dew, the lilac tree was blazing purple, and the tulips were just beyond their peak. My little brother Bobcat was running up the driveway as if fiends were after him. A moment later, he burst into the bedroom. "My van is gone!"

The police arrived ten minutes later. Sergeant Belkor was saying, "You're saying the thief took a beat-up, ancient Econoline van, and left Eric's BMW, an almost-new Scion owned by Mr. and Mrs. Charles, here, and the Prius, ready for the newly-weds' honeymoon. And did they jump-start it, or did you leave the key in the ignition?"

"I don't understand why they took it," moaned Bobcat. "But I know how. I left my keys in my jacket, hanging in the hall."

Sergeant Belkor shook his head. "So the burglar needed a van to get away with the loot, and your keys happened to be handy. Bad luck, son."

Bobcat banged his head with his hands. "And I don't have any insurance except just liability. How'll I get to Burger King for my Monday shift?"

Sergeant Belkor's partner, Venuti, took a call on their radio, said something to Belkor, and left the house. "And the cat. You say the cat woke you up. How did the burglar get a chance to get all that stuff out of the house if the cat was playing watch cat?"

"She's probably senile," muttered Eric.

Bobcat picked Lin Jee up and petted her. "Don't say that. She's a genius cat. That's what my great-grandmother said, and my great-grandmother was a very smart woman."

Of course Granny also claimed Lin Jee could speak English, but that her Siamese cat accent was so bad nobody could understand her.

Sergeant Belkor smiled tolerantly.

"I think I can explain," I said. "She's got a little arthritis, so it probably took her a little longer to climb up the stairs to the bedroom."

Tom said, "Tell them about the sock."

I laughed nervously. "When we stopped letting her outside to hunt, she took to bringing us socks, pretending they were prey. She hasn't done that in two years, but for some reason, this morning—"

Sergeant Belkor stroked Lin Jee between her chocolate velvet ears. The Siamese narrowed her eyes and turned up the volume on her purr. "I'm a cat man myself. Could I see this sock? Might mean something."

Just then Sergeant Venuti returned. "Well, the van mystery is solved. It's parked behind that tall hedge, on the road. Key in the ignition. Engine's still warm."

Bobcat jumped up, but Venuti restrained him. "Not so fast. We found this in the bed of the van." He held out a shard of china: the roof of a bright blue pagoda, fading into exquisite white.

Bobcat turned pale. "That's a piece of my great granny's vase. She left it to my sister."

"Mmm," said Sergeant Belkor. "You want to tell us what happened to the rest of that vase?"

Bobcat looked down at his bare feet and said, "Sir, I have no idea."

Belkor looked at me and Tom. "Are you going to press charges, even if this turns out to be an inside job?"

I swallowed hard. Lin Jee, tense in my arms, had stopped purring.

Tom came downstairs. "The sock is gone. I looked all over the bedroom for it."

Charlie made a pshawing noise. "Cat hid it again."

I didn't think so. Lin Jee had been lazing in my arms since Tom had tossed the sock at me.

"I will press charges," I said, "if my husband agrees. But first I want you to hold everybody in this room, while your partner brings out their shoes. And their socks, too, if he can find them. Especially any gray socks."

"Why?" asked Charlie.

"I would recognize the sock. I think it belongs to the thief."

Lin Jee started purring again.

Sergeant Belkor tried to hide his smile, but I could see he was planning to go along with me.

Ten minutes later, Venuti had assembled four pairs of men's shoes and two pairs of women's on the marble-topped table in our parlor.

"And whose are these?" he said, holding up a pair of ladies' lavender-dyed silk pumps.

Martha said, "They're mine. And that pair of white athletic socks and the Nikes are mine, too. I can't tell if those are my pantyhose. They might be Mary's."

"Those are my pumps," I said. "The white ones. And the off-white pantyhose. Uh, I assume you didn't go into the closet and haul out all my shoes."

"We assume you didn't burglarize your own house for the insurance. But we did look through your bureau. You gave permission. You favor pastels and bright colors, right?"

"Right. And Tom hasn't moved in yet. He only has the shoes he wore to the wedding, plus a pair of plastic flip-flops."

Next, they turned to Eric's shoes. A pair of black socks were folded neatly inside the left shoe. I felt them. Dry.

Then, Charlie's. He too, wore black socks, and though the toes were worn through, they didn't look like the sock Tom had thrown at me.

Bobcat's boots contained no socks at all.

"You came to my wedding with no socks on?"

"Aw, Sis, if you're wearing boots, nobody can tell."

"Boots? To my wedding?" How had I not noticed?

Belkor turned to me. "I'm afraid this doesn't look too good. I have to wonder if your brother has hidden the sock you think the cat brought to you as evidence, plus its mate."

"I didn't!" Bobcat wailed, startling Lin Jee, who jumped out of my arms and ran to hide. "Somebody stole my van and used it to transport all the gifts, and—"

"And who was that someone?" asked Belkor. "Listen, I think your sister might be willing not to press charges, even though I made her promise to do so, if you'll just tell us where you secreted the loot."

"And what you planned to do with it," said Eric.

Bobcat looked stricken. It was one of the darkest moments of my life. "Honey," I said, "if you need money, I mean for anything besides drugs, you know we'd loan it to you."

"Heck," said Tom, "we'd give it to you."

Bobcat straightened and got a hard look. "This just tops it. Not only do I have to work this lousy job to pay off my debts from that car accident, but—Mary, you're my own sister. Are you turning against me?"

The conversation was interrupted by a terrifying Siamese yowl. Lin Jee stood in the middle of the hall door, blue eyes blazing from her velvet mask, a gray sock at her feet.

"That's the sock," I picked it up. It was damp. "The sock Lin Jee brought us was gray. Lin Jee, tell me where you got that sock."

The next few moments were a blur. Lin Jee leapt on Eric. Eric slammed her against the wall, toppling a lamp. Bobcat gathered her up and held her defiantly against himself. "Don't hurt my sister's cat!"

Eric looked at me, breathing hard. A slash of red oozed across his cheek. "She attacked me for no reason."

Lin Jee's tail fluffed to twice its size, and she emitted a terrifying growl, far too big for such a tiny cat.

I went over and examined her. Her eyes were blue, sharp with intelligence, and ablaze with hate. She flinched a bit when I touched her right front leg, but she didn't cry out again.

"Put her down, Bobcat. See if she can walk."

Bobcat put Lin Jee on the floor, and she limped toward the back bedroom. The room where Eric had stayed.

Eric lunged for her, but Bobcat twisted his arm and the two struggled until Belkor separated them.

We followed Lin Jee.

The other gray, damp sock, was behind the radiator.

Sergeant Belkor looked tired. "This is yours, I gather."

Eric said, "No. I don't wear gray. The kid probably hid it there."

Belkor shrugged. "Well, we could get a search warrant for

your apartment. And I think I have reasonable cause to detain you. Please read this and tell me if you understand it."

Eric glanced at the Miranda rights card and snarled, "I know your boss, you know. And the mayor."

Tom said, "Eric, I don't understand. It looks like you wore these socks out when you were gathering up the stuff to take out to Bobcat's van. So you wouldn't wake us up. Then you must have gone out in your stocking feet and gotten the socks wet from dew. Finally, you drove the goods somewhere and stowed them. Otherwise, why did you attack Mary's cat?"

"I didn't! It attacked me!"

Tom and I exchanged sad glances.

"My oldest friend," said Tom. "I guess business school and that fancy job changed you."

"I didn't finish business school. I flunked out. And the job evaporated in early February. I hope you enjoy the food processor. If you ever find it." He angrily wiped his cheek and scowled at the blood on his hand.

"You could tell us where it is," said Tom gently.

"You could go take a flying leap," said Eric.

Lin Jee lay panting on the floor near the radiator. I picked her up, and she was purring through her pain.

Tom said, "You'll pay for the vet bills, too, of course."

"I haven't admitted anything," Eric said.

Sergeant Belkor let me look in Eric's wallet, where I found a receipt for a storage unit only a mile away. The vase, of course, was broken, and we couldn't prove the money in his wallet was ours. He must have planned to do this. How sad.

Lin Jee's leg was broken, and she looked comical limping around with a white bandage around her leg and a stylish E-collar. Eventually, she squeezed out of the E-collar, gnawed the bandage to ribbons, and went back to her post near the furnace. Tom and I bring her upstairs to bed with us every night, a furry warm bundle with sharp blue eyes. Her velvet brown tail twitches in her sleep, as she dreams, no doubt, of hunting mice, blue jays, and evil socks.

And she tells us off frequently about being so stupid as to trust Eric. I can almost understand her accent now. Granny was right. She's really much smarter than the average burglar.

CAT SEZ

Cat sez
What took ya so long, I was hungry.
I sez
Lemme get in the door, will ya? You ain't even done da dishes.

Cat sez
I don't like to get wet, the suds don't taste so good.
I sez, huh.
Ya can't even answer the phone.
I musta rung ten times. Ya coulda turned the oven on.
Goddam cat. Goddam whiny cat.

She stretches, sez
That's the breaks. Ya bring me some livah?

LIVAH!? I sez. Ya can't even turn on the goddam oven.
LIVAH? I oughta put you back on cat chow.
Ain't even paid me back for your Augmentation Operation.

Huh, she sez.
Big deal.

Experiment on innocent felines.

Yeah, I sez.
Shoulda got ya spayed instead.
Why doncha get a job? Ya so goddam smart now.

What? asks the cat. Operate a computer toiminal with these
teeny tiny paws?

Yeah, I sez.
What, ya think they'd hire ya on TV, like Miss Kitty Fantastico?
Ya too ugly, with that split ear, I sez.

Cats can't get jobs, she sez. 'Sgainst the child labor laws. I'm only
three years old.

Too bad ya too ugly to peddle ya tail on the street, I sez.
It's all ya good for.

More'n you are, she sez. Sets in ta licking her front paws, in
between the toes.

I lose it. Goddam cat.
Here, I sez, take the rest of this stinking tuna fish and shove it.
And while ya at it, I sez, get out and don't come back.

She looks at me, insolent-like. Wraps her tail around her.
'Sokay, she sez. I'm gone. Forward my mail, I'll send a man in
the morning for my stuff.

And I'm looking at an empty door frame.

Round New Year, I hear she's moved to Soho. Part of a dance act.
Apache dancers.
Word is, she's suing me. Suing ME—for Wrongful Intelligence.

A SMALL GIFT FROM MIW

I AM MIW. I was named for my mother, also called Miw. All my litter mates were called Miw, too. The Hebrew humans called us a different name, Cha'tool. Some humans had special names for each cat or kitten.

That winter night, long ago, the shepherds laughed and shouted, skipped and ran. Maybe they were going to a feast. Maybe bits of meat might fall to the ground and I could grab scraps of roasted lamb. I myself was too small to catch a lamb.

But the shepherds didn't go to a warm human house. They went to a shed where the cows lived. That was all right. If I waited 'til morning, I might find a human milking a cow and she would squirt warm milk into my mouth. I loved that. After I wandered away from my mother, I lived mostly on mice and voles I caught. Sometimes I could beg food from small humans if I rubbed against their legs and purred.

In the cold shed I saw a human male they called the Old Carpenter, and a female with a human kitten. Human fathers, I don't know why, stay around the human mothers. Cat mothers would get annoyed and drive the males off, but a human mother allows the father to stay and even gives him some of the food she catches.

The amazing part was the human kitten. It radiated a new feeling, happiness and peace, like being with my littermates, my stomach full of milk. Not sleepy. More like chasing my tail, or hunting a moth, or stalking a sunbeam and catching it, then climbing it all the way up to the sun.

Humans came from all over, many humans. They carried gifts for the human kitten. (Humans used a different word: baby. I could never get my tongue around Aramaic. But I understood human words.)

The barn filled with all colors and sizes of humans. Some smelled like spice and wore heavy, bright colored robes. They brought shiny, sparkly gifts. Others wore wool, soft and worn. Humans don't have much fur, so they cut fur off sheep and turn it—somehow—into coats, which they can take off and on. I had seen them dip these coats in water and then put them out in the sun for a while. The coats get softer as they get older and they get holes and patches, too. Water is deadly, so maybe it poisons the coats.

Anyway, the humans with the soft, worn-out wool coats brought useful things, bread and blankets and dried-up fishes.

I went up to a small wool-coat human and asked her politely if I could also bring a gift.

She just said, "What are you meowing about? You'll wake the baby!"

The baby was already awake, though not crying. He was looking around and smiling sweetly, as really nice humans sometimes do. But, young as I was, I knew kittens need their sleep, even human kittens. So I decided I could give the gift of a lullaby.

At my first meow, the girl shushed me. Oh well. I settled down in sphinx position and set up a purr. The baby waved his arms around. I knew I was making him happy.

Two of the shepherds brought soft woolly blankets. Then some strange dark men brought a beautiful red velvety blanket with shiny threads. The red blanket was too thin, and the thick woolly ones fell off the baby. I looked around for the mother and father, but some visitors were telling them about their long trip to get here and how one night it had been cloudy and they couldn't see the guiding star, so they were last to arrive.

I could tell the mother and father wanted to get away and watch over their baby, but they were doing the human thing called "doing homage."

We cats don't do homage unless the high-born is one who has torn off one of our ears, and then, we just avoid that particular high-born and hope he will die soon.

I crept with soft paws into the manger with the human kitten and settled all warm beside him.

The baby and I were nice and cozy now and almost asleep when one of the servants of the rich humans seized me by the scruff of my neck. Somebody was yelling something about fleas and calling me an "unclean animal." One of the servants in fine bright clothes even said I would smother the baby. Then the servant flung me like garbage out into the night.

I sat down and washed thoroughly until the perfume and spice scent of the rude servant was gone. Too bad the sweet scent of the baby was also gone, but I did have standards.

Then I went hunting.

The mouse was a nice fat little fellow, his coat a pretty shade of gray. His eyes were as shiny and bright as the black beads on the rude servant's coat, and his tail was long and graceful. And I was careful not to kill him, just carry him delicately in my jaws, like my mother carried me when I was not much bigger than a mouse.

Humans don't actually eat mice, or at least not unless they are very hungry. Hebrew people like the baby's parents were picky about what they ate. But the baby needed a toy.

I dropped the only slightly injured mouse on the baby's tiny stomach and stood back with pride at my gift. Surely it was better than those boxes of perfume and shiny metal. Maybe the blankets and cakes and dried fish were useful, but a mouse—a nice fresh mouse—it moved! It made squeaky noises! Wasn't that the best present in the whole world?

One of the servants shrieked and then everybody started yelling. A hand—not the baby's kind parents'—grabbed the mouse by its tail, flung it on the floor, and stamped on it.

What a horrid way to say thanks! What a waste of a perfectly good mouse!

Everybody in that barn turned and looked at me.

I sprinted as fast as my four legs would carry me, out the big barn door, away from the manger with the wonderful human baby, out into the cold.

I ran and ran until I reached the top of a hill where nobody would chase me anymore. I looked up. There was a star above the barn, right at the top of the dark heavens. It shone so bright I almost forgot how heartbroken I was that they hadn't let the baby play with the mouse.

———

That was years ago. I am an old cat now, old and canny. My back is not as strong, and I do not see mice quivering in the grasses as well as when I was a sleek new kitten. But I am much smarter.

As my life went on, every so often I would ask other cats, or even dogs or sheep, about what had happened to that Old Carpenter and his sweet wife and the amazing baby. They couldn't speak as well as I can, but I learned the family had gone first to a land called Egypt, which is supposedly where all us cats come from. Then I heard they had gone back to their old home, and the baby had grown up to be a carpenter like his father.

I also heard stories about how brilliant and beloved the Young Carpenter was, and how he had once saved a party by making spoiled grape juice, which the humans inexplicably like instead of water or milk, when it ran out. The humans were beginning to call him by the name of Rabbi.

In my long life, I have been a house cat, when an Egyptian lady lured me with cream and goose liver. I have been a farmer's cat and kept the vermin down so the farm family prospered. I have been a roving, free cat and lived by my wits, sometimes eating mice and even locusts, sometimes rooting through garbage in the middle of the night to find some tidbit that a wealthy centurion had cast away.

I have never had kittens. Perhaps I am some sort of sport, a type of cat that cannot have young, but lives very, very long.

Always, I listened carefully when humans or animals spoke of the Young Carpenter. I would ask where he lived. I learned, at last, of his home with his father, the Old Carpenter, in Galilee.

And so I went there and made myself at home in a cave nearby. No, I did not approach the Old Carpenter's sweet wife. Gentle though she was, I feared that she knew the superstition that cats are creatures of The Adversary. For once, when I was waiting outside the Hebrew temple, I heard an old man, much venerated, say that the only domestic animal not mentioned in the Torah was a cat.

I watched the Young Carpenter's family. The Young Carpenter and the old one took wood and made it into chairs and tables and stools. The mother kept order for the house and their shop.

They were clever and made all the parts fit together perfectly. Their tools were artfully made, handles fastened with leather thongs.

When the family sat down to supper one night, the mother said, "I had to throw out a whole jar of meal. Rats got into it again."

The men nodded and said they would catch the rat and get rid of it.

Another young human, John, was eating supper with them. He grabbed a big kitchen knife and said, "I'll take care of them."

Not a minute later, an enormous rat squeezed out from under a box and scampered across the floor. The human John threw his knife almost as fast as a cat, and the knife sliced through the fat part of the rat's tail and pinned it to the floor. John's eyes blazed with blood-thirst, and he grabbed the rat, tearing the knife from its flesh.

He raised the rat over his head, ready to bash its brains out.

But the Young Carpenter put a hand on his arm. "The rat is only following its nature. It's hungry, and like any animal, it seeks food. It's wrong to kill. Here. I'll put it in this sack and take it out across the river where it will eat grass and insects."

But even with that rat gone, the family's troubles weren't over, for the rat had a dozen daughters, and each of them had another dozen daughters, and I knew these rats were evil. I spent time in the Synagogue and learned about the nature of various animals. The Torah had nothing good to say about rats. Humans were not even allowed to eat them.

Snakes were not well regarded either, but that house had no snakes.

Personally, I was not fond of rats either. A rat killed and ate one of my littermates when she was only a few days old. Another rat bit a human baby in a house where I lived and the baby took a fever and died.

The final straw for the Young Carpenter and his family was one workday when the Old Carpenter raised his adze in order to smooth a spoke on a wheel, the adze flew from his hand, striking John a glancing blow on his cheek. He let out a cry of frustration. The three looked at the adze handle and saw that the leather thong holding the blade to its handle had been chewed through.

"What can we do?" asked the Old Carpenter. "We've made the shop as tight as it can be, and rats still squirm through chinks and gnaw on whatever suits them."

Many years ago, this family had scorned my gift of a small, perfect mouse, a totally inoffensive creature made by their God as a food and a plaything for my kind. I vowed to make them a gift they would truly understand, for I knew which rat was the father of all these rats. I knew if I killed him, his descendant rats would flee.

And so I stalked the unclean, evil animal.

I am not the biggest of cats. And I am also not a young cat in the prime of my strength.

But I am cunning.

A human female I know occasionally gives me bits of cheese

—not my favorite food, but when you live alongside humans, you learn to eat what they throw away.

So the next time I got a bit of cheese (moldy, but never mind), I took it in my jaws, and deposited it near a hole where I knew the rat entered the carpentry shop.

Then I hunkered down and made myself look like a shadow. I pretended to sleep.

When the rat came sniffing after the cheese, I waited until his greed had made him stupid, and in a flash, I snatched him.

He thrashed and twisted his neck around, trying to bite me with tiny, sharp teeth. I shook him, but he kicked at my throat with his powerful back legs. I almost dropped him then, but my jaws were still strong and I had most of my teeth. So I shook him even harder and bashed his head against the ground. He shivered and went still, pretending to be dead.

I was not fooled. I would not put him down.

I would not kill him until the Young Carpenter's family could witness my deed. I did not want them to imagine that I had simply found a dead rat.

They would be so impressed! I trotted around to the door of the shop and stepped proudly inside. My eyes shone as I displayed my prize.

Then, using my utmost strength, I shook the rat until its neck snapped.

The men stared at me. Even the mother stared at me, though she looked a little ill. You can tell this about humans because their eyes grow shiny and they breathe shallow and quick and shrink away from the unclean thing.

I dropped the dead rat at the feet of the Young Carpenter and wove around his legs to make sure he understood that the creature was my kill, my final gift to the baby who had grown to be the Young Carpenter.

Then John approached. I felt danger, and I backed away.

John said, "Cousin, you have said that killing is wrong. You once spared a rat's life—maybe even this same rat. So this animal, this cat, has done an evil thing. Mustn't it die? Shall I seize it and drown it in the river?"

The fur of my back rose and I braced my legs to run. The men had blocked my way out of the shop. I braced myself to dart between their legs and—

But the Young Carpenter squatted so that he was not as frightening as the man John. He held a finger out to me, and I suddenly calmed. I felt the same sweetness as I had when I first saw him, when he was first born and lying in straw. I sniffed his hand, then began to purr.

"This is the creature's nature," said the Young Carpenter. "The rat's nature was to eat our grain and the leather of our tools. We did not kill the rat for following his nature. Now this creature's nature is to catch rats and kill them."

I was affronted. Didn't the Young Carpenter realize that I had killed the rat as my gift to him, because the rabble around his birthplace would not accept any of the gifts I had offered many years ago?

The Young Carpenter stroked the fur between my ears. I purred louder, not able to understand the sense of joy that made me purr.

"I remember you," said the Young Carpenter. "You offered your song, and your warmth, and a live thing you thought I would like as a toy. Yes, I remember."

The mother spoke softly. "The cat that the Kings' servants drove away? This is the same animal?"

"It is," said the Young Carpenter. "And why should it not be our household cat? It has few years left in its little body. Surely we can let it have table scraps and perhaps milk. And it will not kill more rats, because its belly will be full."

"But the dead rat—" said John.

The Young Carpenter picked me up and scratched between my ears. I never let humans pick me up, but this Young Carpenter was different. I purred and purred.

"There will be no more rats here. This cat—its name is Miw,

though you may call it Cha'tool—has done us a service. Believe me, if it lives here with us, we will see no more rats."

John shook his head. "You have said that killing is wrong. The Torah says—"

The Young Carpenter petted me, and said, "Do you presume to speak for my Father, or for me?"

The Young Carpenter put me down gently, then tied the dead rat up in an old bag. I must have been mistaken, but I could swear I heard that rat feebly squeak.

I still live in that house as I grow old.

I think the Young Carpenter, even as a baby, was able to give me this long, long life.

I kill no more rats, maybe because my eyesight is poor, and my hindquarters are weak. Or perhaps because no rat dares come to the house of the carpenters.

NOTES TOWARD A NEW TRAIT AS REVEALED BY CORRELATION AMONG ITEMS OF THE MMMPI

M. PURRZILLO, U. R. A. FERBALL, AND C. KITIRUN

ABSTRACT

THE MAINE MAUSER Multichoice Psychological Index (MMMPI) is used to categorize personality types and disorders. Based on newly found correlations, we propose a new trait, Type F Personality Cluster.

DISCUSSION

Researchers note a puzzling correlation in selected subjects between item 401: *I am seized with terror at the thought of being immersed in water* and item 447: *I bathe several times a day* (Hunter and Pounce, 1968). The authors have discovered a third perplexing correlation, with item 68: *I find it relaxing to torture small animals*. In the present paper, a new trait is proposed, strongly correlated with these and other items in the MMMPI. After rejecting such names as *oral cleanliness fixation, hedonistic sadism,* and *self-induced catatonia*, the authors decided to call the trait *Type F Personality*.

The authors' clinical practices contain patients who appear tormented by their housemates' capricious behavior. We therefore undertook a study of 43 individuals who cohabit with our patients in therapy.

The patients typically remark that "X is driving me crazy" or "I never know what she's going to do next," but exhibit extreme distress if the possibility of severing the relationship is suggested. Clearly, the housemates contribute to a therapeutically negative climate in the homes of these patients.

The authors administered the MMMPI to these 43 housemates in an attempt to recognize traits complementary to the those seen in the patients. We hypothesized a codependency between the anxiety of the patients and the obsessive cleanliness, skittishness, and narcissism described as typical of the housemates.

The researchers requested that the housemates make office appointments in order to respond to the MMMPI. However, we were told by the patients that the housemates "do not travel well," or "would scratch and claw me if I tried to get her into the car."

The researchers recognized immediately the dysfunctional relationship that had developed between these patients and their housemates. However, pragmatism suggested that the test could be taken home and administered in a domestic setting.

Some patients complained that the housemates simply lay down on the form, or attempted to tear it up, or, in one case, urinated on it. However, seven more or less completed answer sheets were returned.

To the researchers' surprise, a clear—if very puzzling—pattern emerged at once. The subjects answered in the affirmative to the following items:

18: *I enjoy throwing up.*
96: *I often stare at spots on the carpet until my eyes cross.*
201: *Among outdoor sports, I much prefer hunting over swimming.*
258: *I sleep over eighteen hours per day.*
397: *Thunder and lightning terrify me.*
437: *I lick my body all over several times a day.*

636: *When company visits, I like to hide under the bed.*

These correlations suggest a personality configuration, the Type F Personality, that could trigger many of the neurotic traits of the patients themselves: most notably coming into therapy sessions with clothing matted with long fibers, and a compulsion to leave the session early in order to buy King's Ransom brand tuna before the deli closes.

One of the researchers (Ferball) suggests that the relationship with the Type F housemates might actually be therapeutic to subjects who suffer from anxiety or attention deficit disorder (ADD). These patients are encouraged to sit quietly for long periods of time when the housemates settle on their laps and prevent them from moving. Kitirun suggests further that the presence of an uncritical bed mate might be a positive force. However, many of the Type F housemates are described as arising in the middle of the night and dashing around knocking over lamps. This could scarcely contribute to the tranquility of an already anxious therapeutic client.

The authors propose the development of a new instrument to measure the Type F Personality, containing the following items:

String and yarn excite me.
I find closed doors personally offensive.
Birdwatching is a favorite hobby of mine.
When I am embarrassed, washing makes me feel better.
I sometimes eat bugs between meals.
I like to play with my food before killing it.

Further studies must include individual interviews with the housemates. The authors plan to undertake such a series of interviews and are applying for federal funding to supply King's Ransom brand tuna.

LYNX STAR: THE SNEAKY INVASION

THE EARTHLING astronomer Johannes Hevelius was right in calling the constellation Lynx, for orbiting one of the stars in this fancifully named cluster is the home planet of a race of intelligent beings who look very much like big cats: large eyes and ears, silky fur, fearsome retractable claws, and beautiful striped tails. Myth has it that this constellation was the location of the star of Bethlehem. Of course the natives of this planet are different from our terrestrial house cats in important ways: for one thing, they can decide whether to go through an open door or not.

The reason they looked like cats will soon become clear. It's more that cats look like them.

These aliens decided that they owned their immediate vicinity of the galaxy, and that segment included Earth. With their seventh sense, they were able to instantaneously perceive events light-years away. And, with a little sleight-of-paw and advanced engineering, they could influence events on planets as distant as Earth.

Like our homey little felines, these aliens believed that they should run everything in their arm of the galaxy to their own liking.

When they discovered humanity, they saw that the race was poorly managed. One ethnicity would subjugate another; one religion would declare war on another. Husbands would suddenly take it in their heads to bludgeon their wives, and vice versa. Children would assault each other to obtain games or trendy shoes or a greasier lunch.

One of the more forward-thinking aliens (his name happened to be Coeurl, but don't hold that against him) called together a clowder of cat-scientists and convinced them that humanity needed to be reformed.

Coeurl's sometime-but-not-always mate, Butterpaw, suggested that a smaller version of themselves could be introduced to planet Earth. Call these creations cats.

Under this plan, when a human was tempted to get up and smash an expensive television, whether because of Fox News or CNN, a small cat would settle itself on the human's lap and purr. The warmth would eventually make the human forget about his destructive urges.

When a mother was tempted to backhand her adolescent daughter for wearing black lipstick and pants cut low to display a skull-bedizened navel ring, a cat would leap into her arms and nuzzle her face.

The aliens realized this same ploy had been attempted by another race of aliens from a planet orbiting the white dwarf called the Pup, the binary companion of the Dog Star. This tiny planet has not been detected by humans, and the planet itself is called by many aliens the Mini-Mutt.

The Dog Star ploy never really worked because the animals the dog aliens sent to Earth decided to worship the Earthlings, and even allowed themselves to be used as attack animals in annoying and inappropriate Earthling wars.

Coeurl and Butterpaw's race took heed of this and made sure their feline invaders would never take orders from anybody.

The plan was very successful. Small alien cats were widely accepted all over the Earth. The Terrans were bamboozled into thinking the little cats had always been there, back to the time of

Egyptian dynasties. Some believe the aliens from Lynx actually did introduce them many centuries earlier, via a time machine.

As this plan unfolded, if a world leader got it in his head to teach some other world leader a lesson with a nuclear weapon, a Siamese kitten would climb on his lap and toy with his necktie until he forgot what he was so exercised about.

Still, humanity had some issues. Butterpaw suggested introducing a protozoan which could alter human behavior. In a human female, the infection (which was otherwise relatively harmless) would prompt her to spend an inordinate amount of time on her clothing and makeup, so she would have no time to get an advanced degree in weapons design. And suppose a human male had a sudden urge to write a computer virus that would so enrage the user that he would assault members of his family and passersby, or possibly starting a drunken brawl at a Chuck E. Cheese kindergarten graduation party. In such a case the infected human male would notice that his Maine Coon kitten needed to be petted. He would suddenly forget what he was doing and start playing Splatoon.

The humans, when they discovered the existence of this protozoan, termed it *Toxoplasma gondii*. Since it had no gross symptoms other than the sneaky psychological ones, and since half the human race, including most of the medical profession, was infected, the terrestrials did very little to counter it. So, human women engineers salivated over Manolo Blahnik high heels instead of working on cold fusion, and men computer scientists just played Catlateral Damage or Exploding Kittens and let their beards grow all scruffy.

But yet, there was the problem of warring religions. Butterpaw's littermate, Floofyskull, pointed out that Catholics and Protestants assaulted each other, radicalized Muslims were attacking Christians, Buddhists oppressed Tamil Hindus, Protestants lashed out against Mormons, and some religions even had one branch of that faith terrorizing another over ghostly matters that nobody sane could verify. And everybody had tried to exterminate Pagans at one time or another.

So, the aliens from the Lynx constellation augmented their feline messengers to pay special attention to religious readers. Soon churches, synagogues, temples, and other places of worship displayed images of their deity attending to a friendly cat. A Christian Nativity scene now included an Egyptian Mau cuddled up to the sacred child. In Buddhist statuary, the Enlightened one had a sleek Thai kitten on his lap. And of course the aliens had already spread the anecdote of the prophet Mohammed, that he cut his robe rather than disturb Muezza, his favorite cat, who was sleeping on the hem. A similar story is told of the Sufi Ahmed ar-Rifa'i, except that he stitched the hem back on his garment when the cat woke and sauntered away. This was so the cat could come back and deposit cat hair all over his robe again.

Although humans were beginning to act more peaceably, as the aliens from the Lynx constellation thought appropriate, there was still too much strife. A quarrel had broken out over somebody yelling "Merry Christmas!" or maybe it was "Happy Holiday!" or more probably "A Blessed Solstice!" The revelers broke off branches of a Christmas (or maybe it was a Yule) tree and whipped each other bloody until somebody pulled the plug on the Star Shower™ and the light-up inflated Grinch and they were plunged into darkness.

Floofyskull had the answer, and by relentless meowing she was able to convince the rest of her race. They needed a deity who would be universally worshipped.

And so FTL ships were dispatched from that planet in the constellation Lynx, bearing enormous animatronic talking statues of Bast. They would land in Times Square, Tiananmen Square, Zawra Park, Trafalgar Square, Piazza San Pietro, Downtown Disney, and a hundred other places of political and spiritual significance.

Bast, as everybody knows, is very motherly, and large, and she purrs deep and loud. She is the goddess of fertility and plenty and love and sexuality and everything else peaceful and delicious that humans enjoy.

DINOSAURS MAY BE ANCESTORS OF MORE THAN BIRDS

Paleontologist Dr. Felix Stalker
today unveiled three specimens
thought to prey
on ancestors of birds.
"Logic says," according to Stalker,
"where there's birds,
there's got to be cats."

First specimen:
Acatasaurus. Originally thought vegetarian,
this long-necked ancestor of the Siamese
probably fed on early fish.
Early aquariums may be discovered
on future digs.

Second:
Velocimouser. This quick-witted,
swift catosaur captured prey
by silent stalking, then pouncing.
Clever and voracious, it
may have gone extinct because caught off guard

taking naps
after dismembering small mammals.

Most controversial specimen:
Purranosaurus Rex. Note long, rapacious teeth.
Also called Thunder Catosaur because of low rumbling sound
emitted after devouring prey
or shredding furniture.
Small front limbs may not have been
as useless as they look.

Dr. Stalker showed bone fragments
of other catosaurs
"too early to categorize,"
he said. "But tentatively named
Triwhiskerops (note pointed structures
either side its head),
Meowasaurus, good mother catosaur,
Prrtadactyl, Kittycoatlus, and *Architsbackterix*,
evolutionary blind alleys
nature abandoned when catosaurs
found they could not leap forty feet.
And finally the ancestor of the domestic feline: *Ankylorubbosaur*."

Dr. Stalker plans next summer
to seek fossils
of a species
believed to prey on catosaurs:
the *Fidonychus*.

WHEN CASSIE AND ME GOT INTO THE FREEZER

MOM WAS out with her weird new boyfriend, the paleo-something guy, and Cassie and I were bored, so we decided to thaw out a kitten to play with. The labels were all in some code, so we just took one out at random, and I warmed it up by putting it in some warm water in the sink, inside a plastic bag with the top open so it could breathe when it woke up. We named it Romulus. It was a fluffy orange one, and it sure was cute, but it kept attacking us, so we figured it needed a playmate.

This time, we peeked inside the wrapper, and we picked out a calico, cause Cassie heard calicos were girls and Romulus and the calico wouldn't be so feisty, him being a boy and her being a girl, sort of like they might be boyfriend and girlfriend cats.

We named her Patchwork. But when Patchwork came awake, she saw Romulus and ran and hid and we couldn't find her. I think she got out through a window in Mom's office. Or maybe she climbed up inside the mastodon model. So we went back and dug out a pair of little black ones at the very bottom of the freezer, my they were so cute, and we figured if there were two of them they wouldn't be scared of the fluffy orange one. Well, they started in fighting with him right away, and Romulus climbed the blinds and tried to hide above the ceiling tiles. So I had to climb up on the lab table and drag him down. He knocked over the cast of the dire wolf skull, but I didn't think Mom would notice since it only got a little crack in it.

I held Romulus, or tried to, anyway. And the two black ones started fighting each other, and we had to lock all three in the mail room so they wouldn't knock over any more casts or models.

So now Cassie and I were alone and still bored, so I said let's thaw out the whole batch. I think there were seventeen altogether. Seventeen is my favorite number, and Cassie says it's sacred to the cat goddess, I think its name is Bast.

Cassie put them in bags in a covered pan and set the hotplate on low, and turned the timer on. We waited and waited, and Cassie was afraid we'd cooked them, but when we uncovered the pan, they all jumped out and some of them ran and hid and others started climbing up our legs and some of them got into the trash and dragged some chicken giblets left over from feeding the monkeys out into the kitchen, and that's when I remembered my ferret, Harry Beest, was in the mail room with the fluffy orange kitten and the two black kittens, and I had left the top off Harry's cage.

Well, I never did find Harry, but that's when Mom came home and guess what? Her new boyfriend Stan was with her, the paleo-guy she'd met on the dig. He had an ice chest with him.

I know, I know, we shouldn't have thawed those kittens out. Mom said they were an experiment and now she won't know how it turned out, since they all ran away. She scolded us really bad, and I promised we won't mess with the things in that ice chest Stan brought.

I did peek, though. The kittens inside were kind of ugly, with big heads, and these really long canine teeth.

YOSHI AND THE DRAGON'S PEARL

THE DRAGON SEIRYU howled up the storm of the century. The roar of the wind battered the cherry trees and whipped petals to the ground, where they lay like the teeth of young maidens.

Yoshi the fish merchant was well and truly lost. The thunder drowned out his ability to think. He bent his back to plod through the almost solid downpour.

He scrabbled into the entrance to a cave. It might have been Shizushi Cave. A half hour ago, the fish merchant had delivered buri and sabi to a fine tourist restaurant, but the violence of the storm had destroyed his sense of direction. He was lost.

Surely the storm would abate. Surely the dragon's anger would be appeased, or the kami would grow bored with its tantrum.

But the storm raged on. Then Yoshi sensed a little pause, as if he was in the eye of the giant tempest.

He pulled his donza around him and shivered. He hated to get soaked any further, but he realized the minute there was a slight break in this torrent, he must dash out into the weather if he was to get home tonight to his clever wife Tomiko.

He poked one toe out into the wet open air, and suddenly

found himself on all fours. He stood back up on his legs, but when he looked down, he saw to his horror that his hands and feet were furnished with fur, and when he reached out to steady himself, claws poked out from the tips of each digit.

Yoshi shook his head, spraying drops of rain to mingle with the downpour. He realized to his horror that his ears were drenched and also enormous, and that his face had sprouted long stiff whiskers, whiskers now dripping cold raindrops.

Oh, by the lord Buddha, he thought, *some mischievous kami has turned me into a cat.* No sooner had he realized this than a huge flaming shape swooped down upon him, and snatched him aloft. Wind whipped his tail like the end of a kite, and wet wind raked his fur.

And as quickly as the nightmare had begun, he was set down roughly in another place, a temple, this one lit by oil flames in beautiful celadon sconces. Still on all fours, he cowered, scrunching his eyes half-closed in fear of a blow from the creature that had seized him.

"Evil kami!" boomed a deafening voice. "Give me back what you have stolen or your days of terrorizing Kyoto will be permanently over."

It was the great dragon, Seiryu.

"Lord Seiryu," meowed Yoshi, raising his cat-yowl to be heard over the storm. "I am not Byakko! I know he is the mischievous tiger-kami, your enemy in all things. I am but Yoshi, a moderately clever fish merchant with a fine wife. I have stolen nothing!"

The great dragon Seiryu coiled his sinuous body down double and put his huge green eye to peer at the little white cat that had been Yoshi. "Hm! I see I was mistaken. When I bespelled you, you did not turn back into an evil tiger, but became a small, wet tomcat. Hm!"

"Please, Lord Seiryu, do me the honor of turning me back into Yoshi the fish merchant."

Lord Dragon Seiryu roared so loudly that, miles away, torii of the shrine of Fushimi Inari all trembled, and some fell down.

"How shall I find my precious pearl? Byakko, the tiger-kami, has stolen it! My precious thunder-ball! My jewel that makes the rain and lightning! With it gone, how can I see the reflection of all that is now and will be?"

Yoshi thought the dragon had done pretty well in the storm-raising business even without his thunder-ball. He licked his flanks in an attempt to get dry. He soon gave up and crept nearer to one of the blazing oil sconces, huddling into a little cat-ball to conserve warmth. He felt as miserable as a wet cat can feel.

Absently, the dragon breathed upon him so he dried off and warmed up. But he was still a cat, and he was not happy with that.

Yoshi asked, "How did you raise this monstrous storm without your great pearl?"

Seiryu roared so angrily that Yoshi dashed and hid behind a vase of lotus blossoms. The dragon spit out his answer without even looking at the poor fish merchant: "Don't ask impudent questions, you insignificant appendage to a tail!"

Then Yoshi had an idea. He crept out from hiding and asked, "Suppose I help you find your pearl?"

Lord Seiryu uncoiled his undulant blue-green body, and turned on Yoshi with a snarl. "How could a miserable wet furball like you help me? The evil tiger-kami has rolled it away like some kind of toy."

"Cats, even god-like tigers, do like to play with balls," Yoshi admitted.

"And Byakko has hidden it!" He let out a roar. Tears shot from his eyes, and the storm grew more intense.

"I can creep into very small places," said Yoshi. "Cats are made so our heads and paws can explore narrow crevices to hunt mice."

The dragon wiped away a tear with his enormous claw. "Maybe," he rumbled, "but how would you ever find it in the first place?"

"With all this thunder and noisy storm, I couldn't," meowed Yoshi. "But cats have the finest hearing of any creature, and if there were silence, maybe I could hear the ball rolling to and fro between Byakko's paws."

"That is all very fine," said Seiryu, calming the storm just a tiny bit, "but even in silence, you would have to know in what part of Kyoto to look."

"Cats talk to each other," meowed Yoshi. He liked cats, even before he had become one. He and Tomiko had a small bobtailed kitten at home, where he devoutly wished he was now. "Haven't you seen them come up to one another and touch noses ever so gently? I will inquire among the cats of Kyoto."

Seiryu thought about this, and the noise of the storm stilled. "Go, then, little Yoshi-cat, and find me my pearl."

Yoshi thought, *Good! I can run away home now, and this powerful dragon will forget me! I will still be a cat, but at least I will be at home with my clever wife, who loves cats.*

He scurried out into the dark, and leapt nimbly over puddles so as not to get his paws wet.

He had gone only a dozen paces before he heard a low chuff that made his blood run cold.

Waiting for him at the end of the path was Byakko the tiger-kami. His yellow eyes glowed with malice, his huge claws, sharp as katana, were fully unsheathed and tapping the wet ground in calculated anticipation.

"Greetings, little Yoshi! You are not the only one with good hearing. The great cats also hear well, especially a tiger who is also a kami."

Yoshi cowered down and made himself small, preparing for the fatal blow.

The tiger-kami raised his paw, claws fully extended.

"Wait!" meowed Yoshi. "Are you not cold and wet after that horrid tempest the dragon Seiryu raised?"

The claws retracted, and Byakko bent his huge head to look at Yoshi. Yoshi could smell the hot breath, like roasted cow, but he knew he must steel his small cat heart.

"If you come to my shop," said Yoshi, "I can brew hot tea for you. You can dry off on our nice tatami, and my wife will bring you a fine big fish."

"I do not drink tea," said Byakko, "but a big fish would be delicious. It must, of course, be a very big fish."

Yoshi led Byakko through the rain-soaked streets of Kyoto. Geisha and vendors shrank from the sight of the tiny pussycat leading the enormous tiger-kami. Shopkeepers peeked from behind the shutters of their shops at the incredible sight, for the tiger-kami had almost never shown his face to mere mortals in Kyoto before.

Yoshi, in the meantime, wracked his brain for a plan. He was a cat, and his mind no longer worked like a man's, but like a cat's. He did not have a long memory anymore, nor could he work sums, nor did he remember the beautiful poetry he had written for his wife. Instead, he mentally composed this haiku in her honor:

meow meow me
ow, meow, meow, meow.
meow meow prrrrt.

He still had the slyness of a cat, and that would have to serve him.

When he arrived at his home, Tomiko did not recognize him at first. When he said he was her husband, she seemed not to believe him. Partly that was because he was meowing instead of speaking Japanese.

But the tiger-kami turned all his terrifying kami charisma into charm, and she reluctantly opened the door to the enormous tiger-being and the polite white cat. She began to believe it was Yoshi.

Tomiko was a very clever woman, perhaps even more clever than Yoshi, and her sensitive ear began to interpret Yoshi's purrs and mews.

After Byakko squeezed his monstrous body into their spacious home, Tomiko plied the terrifying kami with saki and plum wine, and soon he was quite mellow. She poured only tiny sips for her cat-husband and herself, and Yoshi lapped it delicately.

While the tiger-kami curled on their tatami, Yoshi trotted into the kitchen to conspire with Tomiko, on pretext of preparing the great fish.

"It is such a shame this fine fish is raw!" said Tomiko when they returned. "It is a carp, and not suitable for serving as sashimi."

"And we have no fire," said Yoshi sadly. "Oh, great tiger-kami, have you any way to help us cook this fine fish?"

The tiger-kami thought and thought. He had been carrying Lord Seiryu's great pearl in the sleeve of his kimono, and he said, "I have this lightning ball. I can make a flash that will sear that fish perfectly."

The minute Byakko produced Seiryu's pearl, Yoshi leaped on his head and scratched at his eyes. Tomiko, terrified but brave, threw the remaining plum wine in the tiger-kami's face.

Byakko dropped the pearl from his huge paws, and Yoshi, who was very small, snatched it and rolled it out a crack under the gate, into the street, beneath carriages and through canals and in the narrow pathways of shrines that the huge clumsy tiger-kami couldn't follow.

Yoshi, carrying the pearl in his mouth, scurried through the Golden Pavilion, and careened through the interior maze. The tiger-kami, as delighted with precious metal as he was by the pearl, was so dazzled by the gold leaf that he got lost in the interior of the temple and upset many priceless screens trying to get out.

By the time the tiger-kami got disentangled, Yoshi noticed a retired geisha playing with her akita puppy in a garden filled with irises, trembling from raindrops, the delicate color of the kimono of the classic heroine Murasaki. Yoshi, who had recently been a man, did not fear dogs, so he pussyfooted up and rubbed his ears against the lady's tabi, purring hypnotically. Charmed, the geisha tried to pick the Yoshi-cat up to hold on her lap, but he squirmed free of her grasp and hid under her kimono. She found this quite amusing.

The tiger-kami, big and powerful though he was, was still part cat, and had a dog phobia, and so when he saw the akita puppy, he steered clear and sped onward, thinking Yoshi must also be afraid of dogs, and so be cowering somewhere in a nearby Buddhist cemetery.

When the coast was clear, Yoshi slunk out from under the folds of the kimono, shook his ears, and streaked off carrying the pearl, favoring paths across overgrown gardens, through stands of bamboo, over tiny koi ponds.

He bounded through rain-streaked streets, paws barely touching the ground, with the precious pearl clutched in his mouth. Please remember that this pearl was magical and could change sizes depending on the situation. And in this situation, it liked the warm, pink interior of Yoshi's mouth, with its hot tongue, abrasive like the irritant that had made it grow in that magical oyster's shell.

As a cat, Yoshi could always find his way, and in less time than it took for a tea ceremony, he was back in Seiryu's temple.

The Lord Dragon Seiryu was overjoyed. He popped the pearl into the sleeve of his own kimono and set a magic spell around his temple. Thus, Byakko could only roar his frustration outside.

Yoshi finished licking his paws dry. "Now will you turn me back into a fish merchant?" Yoshi asked.

"Oh, you know we kami are a fickle bunch," said the Lord Dragon Seiryu. "I will allow you to go home, and I will allow you three boons. But one of them will not be to return to your original form."

"Why not?" yowled Yoshi.

"Because I might need you again as a cat."

Yoshi yowled and screeched and hissed, but nothing could change the dragon's mind. So, he meowed his three wishes.

The first was wealth. The dragon gave him a coin which would magically attract more coins, and she attached it to a red collar which he would always wear.

Yoshi then wished for luck, and the dragon gave him a bell he could ring to attract luck.

Finally, Yoshi wished to attract business for his fish-shop, and the dragon told him that whenever he raised his right paw and moved it in a come-hither motion, customers would flock to his door. And when he raised his left paw and beckoned, those customers would open their purses and buy, buy, buy.

He told Yoshi that henceforth all of Kyoto, and all of Japan, and eventually all the world would call him Maneki Neko, and that statues of him would beckon customers in every Japanese and Chinese shop in the world.

The dragon then sent him home to his clever wife Tomiko. She would miss his human kisses, but she would hold him in her lap and pet him while she read poetry he had written when he was human. And every day, in their fish-shop, he would beckon with each of his paws and bring them luck and wealth.

And he would purr. *A prettier sound*, Tomiko thought, *than that horrible storm that wracked their shop the day Yoshi changed.*

MORE WAYS TO TELL IF YOUR CAT IS A SPACE ALIEN

1. Your cat came from a pet store in Roswell, New Mexico.

2. You find long-distance charges on your telephone bill to area codes the operator has never heard of.

3. You come home to find your cat walking on the ceiling, and your cat just looks at you and says, "Yeah, so?"

4. Your cat goes hunting and brings you home a Little Green Mouse.

5. Your cat's eyes glow in the dark. Even when they're closed.

6. When you scratch your cat behind the ears, you notice she has antennae.

7. Your cat volunteers to remove your brain.

8. You agree to have your cat remove your brain.

9. Your cat can program your computer better than you can.

10. Your cat can program your computer better than your ten-year-old kid can.

11. You discover that your cat has a glitzier Web page than you do.

12. You discover your cat has put you up for adoption on the Internet.

13. UPS arrives at your front door with a cage to take you to your new owner—on TRAPPIST-1e.

PURPLE

OUT OF PURE KITTENISH IGNORANCE, Heaven's first and only kitten angel committed the unspeakable.

The kitten had been admitted by mistake. A little girl named Elvira in Cleveland, Tennessee, had prayed for its soul, and since its name had been Joseph Patrick Michael Thomas Stephen Jesus-Marie Francis Antony Benedict Anselm John Edward, somebody thought it was a human baby.

This kitten, which angels had dyed purple, behaved ignorantly. It meowed instead of singing and threw up hairballs on a fine oriental carpet in a cathedral. One day it killed an innocent mouse angel within the very sacristy of the biggest cathedral in Heaven.

Had it thought the mouse was immortal? No. The kitten didn't even know what death was. Mice were common in Heaven, due to a legal arrangement with a Florida theme park.

So, the angel gardener Bastael demoted it, and cut off its wings, snip, snip, with a pair of hedge-trimmers, right at the shoulder blades.

Now the kitten looked very ordinary, except that it was still purple and had turquoise eyes, with a black nose, three black pads, and one pink pad on its left front paw. As a supernatural being, the kitten healed very fast.

And since it was rattle-brained, it forgot the pain of being wing-clipped, though when it was staring at a cloud, sometimes it would feel a horrid itch between its shoulder blades, and it would lick frantically, trying to remove an imaginary flea.

It even forgot that it had lost its ability to fly.

And so, the angel kitten eventually stepped off the golden pavement into a cloud, and sank and sank and sank until it came to Earth.

It landed in the middle of Route I 71 Southbound, at 4:27 AM on a Saturday, somewhere near Strongsville, Ohio. It still had a lot of angelic buoyancy, so it landed *ka-thunk*, not with a squishy fatal encore smack. On its feet.

The first thing the kitten noticed was that it was quite dark. The kitten was used to Heaven, with lights on all the time, beautiful iridescent glass chandeliers and soft candles scented with lavender, pink and blue neon twisted into uplifting words like PEACE and LOVE and CHOCOLATE ÉCLAIR. Of course, the kitten couldn't read these, because it had a brain the size of an apricot, but it had gotten used to the constant soft glow of everything.

The second thing the kitten noticed was that the surface was cold and hard, unlike the carpet and gold-inlaid floors of Heaven, which were supernaturally softened for tender angel feet.

The third thing the kitten noticed was two blinding lights thundering toward it at breakneck speed.

———————

Bambi Russolini had been driving a truck for thirteen years, and hated it. Born an Italian American Princess, she had a degree in social work, but back when she was ten, her mother had fallen in love with a Polish guy from Akron.

Bambi, a tiny thing, needed special pedals to shift and brake the damn Peterbilt. Oh, it was a nice truck. Her stepfather had tried to woo her affections away from her father by providing this alternative livelihood. Her real father had paid her way all through the New School, but what good was that? There was no money in social work.

Not that truck driving paid much better. But her stepfather had willed the truck to her mother, and those two had been killed, together, in a different truck, a Ford pickup carrying rutabagas. Her stepfather had died instantly, and so her mother had inherited the Peterbilt. Her mother, unfortunately, was mentally impaired by a head injury, and had spent her last fifteen years collecting stray cats.

Bambi hated cats. They smelled, they rubbed their nasty little noses up against you, and they tried to crawl into bed with you and sit on your chest. They confused Bambi with her mother, and when her mother had died, Bambi had shooed them all into the garage, turned on the car engine, and come back four hours later with a roll of garbage bags.

Somebody had freed the cats in time to save them, but that's a different tale.

The purple kitten angel was so frightened at the huge glaring eyes and the roar of—what? A dog the size of God's throne?—that it lost control of its bladder.

The huge eyes loomed bigger and bigger and finally the kitten flattened its ears and squinched close its turquoise eyes and prepared for pain and death. Again.

The first time the kitten angel had been killed, it had attempted to fly from a third-story window. Ordinarily, it might have survived such a fall, but the hummingbird it was chasing had risen up from a reflecting pond that the apartment window overlooked. The kitten angel had fallen into the pond, been stunned momentarily, and drowned. Such is the short life of careless kittens.

Somehow, the kitten angel had always, from birth, assumed it could fly. That was why it was such a disappointment when Bastael had snipped off its wings.

So now, at the last minute, the kitten angel moved its shoulder blades and tried to flap its phantom wings.

But it was no use. The two devil-dog lights were upon it, and the roar and jitter drowned its senses.

Therefore, it was surprised, when the growling stopped, to discover itself still on the pavement, albeit in a warm pungent puddle. If you had an accident in Heaven, the heavenly pavement would just sop it up and convert it to cloud-vapor, odorless and light as steam. But the puddle was still here.

By this, the kitten angel knew it was still on Earth. It unfolded from its crouching position and shook each paw. None of them hurt, although all four were damp.

It sneaked a look at where the glowing eyes had gone. They had turned into red eyes, small red eyes, glowing in the dark. They hovered motionless, then slowly moved back toward the kitten angel.

This time the kitten angel didn't hesitate—it ran for the grass and crouched down. Should it run into the thicket beyond the ditch? Perhaps worse monsters lurked there.

So it watched, fascinated, as the big truck—the kitten now remembered about trucks, having seen some on its way from the pound to Elvira's home—stopped.

A human got out.

The kitten angel thought humans were supposed to be friendly, at least the non-cat-eating breed of human.

This one was small for a human, and wore red leather pants, a pair of amber glasses, a cap that said WHISKY-BENT AND HELL-BOUND, and a pink fuzzy sweater.

"Something in the road," this human said to itself.

The kitten angel squinched down, just its ears and eyes showing above the edge of the ditch.

"Kittykittykitty," said the human, and made wriggling motions with her fingers.

(It must be a she human, judging by the earrings. Big gold hoops.)

The angel kitten had never been able to resist wriggling fingers. Moreover, the human smelled interesting. Lavender, smoke, and a touch of tuna salad sandwich.

So, the angel kitten crept out of the grass and sniffed the human's fingers delicately.

Tuna salad sandwich. Definitely.

Like Elvira, his little girl back in Cleveland.

So the kitten stroked its whiskers along the human's red leather pant legs, which also smelled good, although the kitten had never smelled leather before, except on people's shoes.

It had been taught by its mother that the way to colonize humans is to rub one's scent on them, so you can identify them again in case they change clothing. This doesn't really work, because when they change clothing, the fresh clothes won't have one's scent, but the kitten and his mother didn't know that.

Next, you look unutterably cute.

The proper way to do this is to look up with your eyes as wide as possible, cocking your head to one side, and raise one paw as if to shake hands.

"Aren't you adorable," said the human. "Just freaking adorable."

And the angel kitten felt a hand scoop under its belly and lift it into the air.

The technique of imprinting humans at this point requires a deep, satisfied, trusting purr. The angel kitten tuned up and gave forth: *prrrrrrrrrRRRRRRRRR.*

"Yeeesss," said the human. "Out here trying to grow up and make more adorable little kittens. The humane society would adopt you out, and no doubt somebody would promise oh-so-sincerely to neuter you. But Auntie Bambi has her own kitty birth control plan. Although I do hate to get my pillowcase all bloody."

The kitten felt there was something in these words that should alert it to danger, and it stopped purring.

It did consider scratching the human and running into the woods. But who knew what was in those woods? Dogs, maybe, or more trucks with big glowing eyes.

"Wait," said the human, as she got closer to the truck. "What color are you?"

She held the kitten angel in front of the headlights of the truck.

"Purple? What the freaking blazes kind of color is purple for a cat? Somebody dyed you?"

The kitten angel thought dyed meant killed, and it got really scared. It struggled, but the human had its back paws firmly in her right hand, and no matter how it twisted, it couldn't get at her bare skin to attack.

"No, wait. That isn't dye. Damn if you're not purple. Let me think about this."

She climbed up into the truck and forced the kitten into a cardboard box.

"Shall I take you to a breeder to see if you're worth something as a stud cat or a breeding female? That would mean more cats in the world. There might be money in it, though. Or, I could just take you straight to the taxidermist."

"Breeder? Taxidermist? Breeder? Taxidermist?" She kept that litany up as she drove away.

The dark, cold room smelled of something that the kitten knew was bad. It was the stuff that dripped out of the bottom of the truck. The human called Bambi dipped a rag in some of that stuff and rubbed the kitten's fur. Then she muttered, "I'll be damned. It's real."

The stuff on the kitten's fur burned, and it licked at it. But it tasted horrible and made it sneeze, so it just avoided that part of its fur when it bathed from then on.

Every so often Bambi would come in and give the kitten more water and food. The food was sometimes good, sometimes horrible. Sometimes the kitten got the remains of a sandwich. It could eat the meat part, and sometimes it got so hungry it would eat the bread, but the sour stuff on the bread hurt its tongue, and was hard to nibble around.

Once there was a long time between foods. The kitten cried after a while, its belly hurt so much. The human called Bambi came in and shook its cage hard, and the kitten bounced around and bruised its jaw. After that, it didn't cry when it was hungry.

A small human came in the garage. The kitten had learned that small humans were sometimes dangerous, but easier to charm. So it meowed as prettily as it could, and when the small human came over, it rubbed its face against the fingers the small human stuck in the cage.

"Oooh, way cute!" said the small human. "My name is Trevin. Oh, look, you're purple! I never knew cats came in that color. Is your name Purple?"

Purple. A good name. Easier to remember than Joseph Patrick Michael Thomas Stephen Jesus-Marie Francis Antony Benedict Anselm John Edward, which took forever to say, and therefore meant the kitten got to its food dish (back when it was a pre-angelic kitten) way before the food arrived. Purple.

Purple purred and patted the small human Trevin on the back of his hand.

"I bet Aunty is going to give you to me for my birthday," said Trevin. "Would you like to be my kitty?"

Purple turned up the volume on the purr to frantic.

"Here, kitty. See, this is my helicopter. Want to see it fly?"

A bird sprang from the boy's hands. No, not a bird. A flashing, sparkling thing, delicious to spring upon. Forgetting hunger and thirst, Purple stood on hind legs and pawed at the cage bars. If only! If only! It was the most beautiful, it danced in the air, it needed to be swatted down—

It flew back to the boy's hands.

"Better not let on that I saw you. My birthday isn't until November."

The garage door rolled up. Trevin looked startled and darted out through the side door.

The light from the sun dazzled Purple's eyes. Purple felt its cage being lifted up, and found itself in a light-drenched, chilly open space. Birds chirped, wheedling to be played with. Green leaves waved above. Then the cage, with Purple, lurched out into cold, windy space.

"Where?" asked Purple repeatedly. It sounded more like "Gneyrrr?" but there was nobody around to answer its question, so it didn't matter.

After a long, cold, bumpy ride, Purple again felt the cage lifted up and carried into a dark, smelly place. Dead things were in here, and also some sharp non-animal smells.

A male human said, "Bambi, you old whore. What you got there? I thought you hated cats."

"I do, you foul-mouthed old fool. You know that ugly sword-fish you've got over the tool bench in your garage? That Eleanor won't let you bring in the house?"

"I could bring it in if I wanted. I like it out there."

"Whatever! Can you give me the number of the taxidermist that did that fish for you?"

"Sure! He's in the directory: Tex Tackle and Taxidermy. You're not planning to have that cat—"

"MYOB, Orville. I don't tell Eleanor about your Thursday night movie club, you don't ask about my cat."

Somebody picked the cage up and plunked it down hard. A bright light made Purple blink. A very old human with breath that smelled like rotten smoked meat peered in the cage. "Bambi, did you spray-paint this kitten?"

"Orville, I swear, keep butting in my affairs, I'll tell Eleanor what kind of movies you old fart buddies watch."

———

Purple grabbed on with its claws as the human woman swung the cage back into the bed of the pickup. The truck jolted along until she came to another stop. She came around to the back and looked in at Purple. Purple still liked her gold earrings. Fun to bat around. But the rest of her wasn't nice. Purple wondered if she was going to let that small human play with it. That could be good or bad.

That long word worried Purple: taxidermist. But Purple had a short attention span and forgot about anything except that the cage was getting insanely boring. Several times, Purple had seen flies, just beyond reach. Also, it hadn't had a chance to dash around knocking things over for about a hundred years.

Just about the time Purple had gotten fascinated by some ants it could see in the bed of the truck, the human came back, this time with a female human with a smooth face. She smelled like hand lotion with a lot of cat smells, too. She put a finger inside the cage, and Purple rubbed his chin on it.

"Mrs. Russolini, my sense of humor is wearing thin today. Someone has obviously done something to this poor animal, and I'm about ready to report you to the ASPCA." The smooth face loomed closer to the cage, and Purple slow-blinked her. "My, that is an unusual color. You didn't do anything to its eyes, did you? Like put food coloring in them?"

Bambi said, "The cat is actually purple. I tried to wash it off, but it's in the fur."

"I see you did. With gasoline. I wonder the poor thing is still alive."

The cage snapped open and Purple tried to make a dash for it. A smell of other cats, lots of them. Cats to hide among.

The smooth-faced woman's strong hands lifted Purple's tail. "It's a male, incidentally. The answer is, I'll take this kitten off your hands and make sure it gets a good home. I won't breed it, though. My queens are all champions, and I can't breed them with another champion after they've been bred to a mongrel."

"How much will you give me for it?"

"Twenty dollars. And that's only because I'm afraid of what will happen to it if I don't take it."

"Please don't insult me," said Bambi. "You'll undoubtedly mate it and make your first million that way. Think of what happened to the breeders that got that ugly skin-disease breed started."

"Sphynxes? Please, Mrs. Russolini! This cat is a stray. I have no idea what genetic defects it has. But I won't let you abuse—"

Suddenly Purple felt four hands on its body, each pair tugging in a different direction. It bit down, hard, on the closest finger.

"Demon!" barked the smooth-faced woman.

Purple felt himself shoved back into the cage. He circled around and around, hissing and lashing his tail. Really scared.

After the truck started moving again, Purple calmed down and mulled over what he had just heard.

He was a male. He hadn't been sure he was male. He thought maybe he was, but this woman must know.

After a lot of lurching and bumping, the truck stopped again. Bambi came around the back of the truck with a big paper that she unfolded and unfolded and unfolded. She spread the paper out on the fender and pulled out a white tube. She put fire to the tube and made a smell that made Purple cough.

"I thought Route 224 joined up 360 around here, but what the hell. I can't take the eighteen-wheeler on these blue highways, so

I don't know. What are you looking at?" She pushed her face at Purple. He darted to the back of the cage.

"The taxidermist seems to be in Baconsburg. Doesn't sound kosher."

Purple would like some water. He hadn't had any since the garage, and the small human named Trevin. Every so often he accidentally licked the place Bambi had rubbed the gasoline, so his tongue really needed water.

Bambi inhaled deeply on the white tube and blew smoke at Purple. He tried to catch the smoke, but it wasn't like heavenly clouds, which you could play with. "Jesus Mary Joseph, I don't feel so hot. I'm probably allergic to cats." She started coughing.

She coughed for a long time. Then she lit up another white tube and smoked, coughing. Finally, she sat down on the gravel by the truck.

"Let me rest a moment."

She laid her head against the rubbery round thing and closed her eyes.

———

Purple didn't think Bambi was planning to be particularly good to him, but she had given him the remains of several tuna sandwiches, and some water. Now he wanted both of those things. He would purr extra loud if only Bambi would get up and take him back to the garage with the water.

Purring didn't do any good.

———

Purple got cold after a while. He curled up in the tiniest ball he could and went to sleep. When he woke up, he was even more thirsty, and still cold.

Then after a while he got very hot, as the bright sun shone in his cage. He tried to get into some shade, but the sun followed him wherever he went.

He heard big monsters passing on the road. He decided these must be like the monster that had brought Bambi.

He forgot about being hungry, but he was very thirsty. The temptation to groom that patch of gasoline from his flank went away completely.

Then, as he was lying in the bottom of the cage with his sides heaving and his eyes stuck shut, a loud wailing noise came. Like a meow, but like from a tiger-cat a hundred times as big as Purple.

Red and blue lights flashed and a shadow passed briefly over the cage.

"Dead, all right," said a deep human voice. "Too bad somebody didn't call it in earlier."

"Aw, you know, trucks parked along here all the time. She's not visible from the road."

"Meeeee!" shrieked Purple. But humans don't have very good hearing, and Purple's voice was rusty from thirst.

"Anybody reported her missing?"

"I'll check." Sounds of feet moving. "Yeah, her sister-in-law called it in. Victim's named Bambi Russolini. Said the eight-year-old nephew wondered why she hadn't come back."

Large hands, smelling harsh and clean, opened the cage and grabbed Purple by the scruff. A large face, half covered with black, curly fur, said, "What the heck is this?"

Purple saw his chance. He dug in with his back claws and swiped with his front. The large hands dropped him. He landed, dazed for a fraction of a second, then darted, dodging between big, heavy boots, toward the woods.

Bambi woke up behind the wheel of her rig. No, no, it *wasn't* her rig. It was a big Volvo rig, the nicest model she'd ever seen.

Automatic transmission, power steering, red leather bucket seats, air bags. From behind her she heard the dim shrieking and meowing and purring of her load. It sounded like a million cats.

Disoriented, she realized she was in a line of trucks, all ready to move into a weigh station.

She turned on the radio. All she could hear was the sound of breathy, high, sweet singing, all in some language she didn't understand. Latin? Greek? Hebrew? Sanskrit?

She turned on the CB. More of the same music. She took a deep breath—or tried to—it seemed she no longer could breathe.

She said, "Anybody know how much longer we'll be here?"

A deep, resonant voice said, "Your soul will be processed in the order in which it was received. Please have your conscience ready for inspection when the officer reaches your rig."

She tapped her fingers on the wheel, noticing that they no longer made any noise. She reached for her cigs, but she seemed to be wearing a white coverall with no pockets. And no cigs.

Shortly, a face appeared at her window and a large, exquisitely manicured hand tapped on the glass.

She realized the officer must either be eight feet tall, or he was standing on a stepladder. She wasn't sure if he was male or female. He or she was beautiful, with smooth skin that seemed luminescent. The hair was long and blond, and the eyes were ancient, and yet unsullied by pain.

"Please show me see your license, your log, and your conscience," the officer said.

"Am I dead?"

The officer held out a beautiful, slim hand for her paperwork. "Yes, as a matter of fact, you are. Ischemic stroke. There are no Virginia Slims in Heaven."

She gripped the steering wheel and felt huge, hot tears run down her face.

"No need to grieve and sorrow in this place of eternal rapture," he said. "We meet you on God's golden shore."

"I don't know, I don't know," she blubbered. "I don't know where my freaking conscience is."

"Glove box," he said.

On the sleeve of her white coverall, she wiped a blob of snot that threatened to run down her lip and into her mouth. She reached over and retrieved a white leatherette binder full of papers, then handed it to the officer.

He (she decided the officer was a male, just like that damned purple cat that had brought her to this awful pass) took the papers and began reading, quickly and yet with great attention.

"Ah, I see you are a woman of constant sorrow," he said. "Troubles all your life."

She nodded emphatically, and the tears flowed even heavier.

"Beloved parents. Gone, gone, gone," he said. "Then the beloved husband. Never really materialized. Then the high cost of maintaining a rig. No children. You coveted them, I see, but it's way too late even to adopt. Might have helped, incidentally, if it's any comfort to you." He continued thumbing through the papers. "Sorrow, sorrow, sorrow."

"I'm dead!" she shrieked. "I wanted to pay off my rig! I wanted to find out if Orville really watched porn movies with his buddies or just played Canasta! I wanted to finish that last Stephen King novel! I wanted grandchildren!"

"These seem all in order, Candidate Bambi. You can take them—" but the officer stopped. "Who is Joseph Patrick Michael Thomas Stephen Jesus-Marie Francis Antony Benedict Anselm John Edward?"

"What? What kind of a freaking name is that?"

"He was also called Purple."

Bambi had a sudden, horrid suspicion. "He wasn't a cat, was he?"

"Yes, yes, he was. You put gasoline on his fur, and you were planning to have him stuffed."

She was speechless.

Purple crouched in the ditch at the side of the road. The two men called for him, halfheartedly, but they were busy. Probably had to take the woman called Bambi off to see her friend Orville, or maybe to the taxidermist, whatever a taxidermist was.

She'd have to do it without Purple.

At the weigh station, two more of those enormous officers came up to Bambi's rig and opened the door. Their beauty brought fresh tears to her eyes. Through the rainbow of her tears, she saw they had huge, translucent wings, which they periodically fluffed up and then settled around their shoulders.

One of them had blue eyes and a long, noble nose like her father's. The other had a short nose and curly, reddish hair. Also slit pupils. Like a snake's eyes. Like a cat's eyes.

She had led an exemplary life, she was sure.

But maybe God had not appointed her the Chief Agent of Feline Birth Control for Northeast Ohio. Maybe that had been a mistake. Her insides turned over and made her sick. Yes, she knew even at the time that Feline Birth Control à la Pillowcase and Exhaust Fumes was not God's master plan.

It had seemed so tidy at the time.

"Bambi," said the magistrate. He was wearing a judge's robes, except they were all white, not black. He sat behind a desk in a chair about ten feet off the ground, but the room (immense and whitewashed, except for the doors to the restrooms, which said, THE UNNECESSARY, and were mirrored) held a number of television monitors, probably for those who, like Bambi, were too frightened to look him in the eye. In each monitor, his smooth and noble visage pronounced the exact same words.

"You have had many sorrows, and you have done many ill

deeds, as have most mortals. But we have selected one deed, though it may seem arbitrary, for you to redress."

She repressed her sobs. Sobbing would be contempt of court, she was sure.

"You have unfinished business on the Earth. You will be allowed a six-month pass in order to compensate for the cruelty perpetrated on a number of harmless beings, but most signally to one who had once aspired to divine favor, one Joseph Patrick Michael Thomas Stephen Jesus-Marie Francis Antony Benedict Anselm John Edward."

She didn't dare ask, but still she wondered. How did he get that freaking name?

"Also known as Purple. Named by a small girl in Cleveland, Tennessee, and later by your own nephew, Trevin."

She slowly raised her mascara-streaked face to the magistrate.

The two officers who had brought her moved to each side of her, and took her arms, consolingly, she thought, though they didn't seem to be planning to help her evade her fate.

"Find him," said the magistrate. "You will be judged by what you do then."

The bailiff came forward with a transparent bag, containing, she could see, red leather pants, a pink cashmere sweater, a baseball cap saying WHISKY-BENT AND HELL-BOUND, and a pair of large gold hoop earrings. He handed her the bag. "May the circle be unbroken."

A wind swept through the huge room, and Bambi looked behind her. A door big enough to drive her rig through had slid open.

Beyond yawned clouds and stars.

The two officers guided her gently, firmly toward the door.

"I can't fly!" she screamed. Falling through cold, dark air.

Bambi woke in sodden pain. Her arms and legs didn't move, and her chest hurt like a son of a bitch. She vaguely remembered what had happened in Heaven, but she could see that now she was in a hospital. *I'm in a story,* she thought. *In the next part of the story I'm supposed to find that damned cat and pretend it saved my freaking life and then go all soft and mushy like Ebenezer Scrooge.* Her next thought was: *I can't, though. That damned animal gave me that stroke.*

When the candy striper came in, Bambi opened her mouth to ask what had happened.

But nothing came out.

"You're going to be okay, Sweetie," said the candy striper. "If you're feeling up to it, we've got a surprise for you. My daddy is going to bring in something so cool!"

All afternoon Bambi tried to talk. But the stroke had done something permanent to her. She could only think. Not addled thoughts: very clear ones. But she couldn't say a thing.

Bambi's sister, Robin, came in while she was pretending to be asleep, trying to work out what had happened.

The male nurse said, "Good candidate for therapy, but don't expect miracles."

Robin sounded weary. "I don't know how I'll tell my son. He loved her. He kept saying she was going to give him a wonderful birthday present. Now this."

The nurse said, "Speaking of which, here comes our pet therapy team." He rolled Bambi's bed to a semi-sitting position. Bambi pretended to wake up.

A beefy man in a red ball cap peeked in the door. He approached, carrying something in a blanket.

"Here. This is Twickle, our therapy kitten." He leaned closer and whispered mock-conspiratorially. "Don't tell him he's not a mutant. He doesn't realize the color will grow out."

They put it on her lap, though it tried to claw free. When it calmed a bit, held in place by The Fireman, Bambi was weeping.

Tears of rage.

Bambi had felt loss her whole life. She had lost her father and her stepfather. She had lost her mother to dementia. She had lost her dream of marrying some subservient but virile man who would cook, clean, rub her back, and also bring home the bacon.

And now she had lost her ability to speak. Every day they would wheel her, over her strong objections, down to that room that looked like a kindergarten classroom. Some damn woman in jeans and a tee shirt would be waiting, with cards and some crappy idea of putting her left hand, the one that worked, in an oven mitt and forcing her to try to talk, even though it wasn't working, would never work again. "Bird! Say Bird, Mrs. Russolini! See the bird fly?"

Bambi couldn't even crawl. What did she want to do with flying?

The only thing Bambi had not lost was Trevin. Bambi had never gotten along very well with her sister Robin, but Trevin never noticed that his aunt was a bitch.

"You've got insurance for thirty days here," Robin announced. "Then it's warehouse time for you."

"Auntie," said Trevin, who had been lurking in the hallway, "what happened to the kitten you were going to give me for my birthday?"

After those first visits, Robin dropped Trevin off at the front door of the rehab hospital. It wasn't clear how he got past the front desk; the receptionist may have thought he was with some other adult. Anyway, Trevin came by several times a week after school and told her about TV shows he'd seen and games he played.

The day after Trevin's birthday, he brought a bright silver helium balloon from his party.

"Look, Aunt Bambi. It wants to go up and up. If I let it, it would go above the ceiling and all the way up to Heaven."

Bambi was surprised and dismayed to think of her nephew knowing about Heaven, especially since she'd been there and didn't look forward to her next visit. She could tell him things about Heaven.

Purple liked his new house. He had to take rides in a car sometimes so he could sit on humans and purr. They seemed to like it when he purred, and purring wasn't hard. In fact, when he was tired, it was easy to fall asleep on one of those humans. He didn't like the lady who had put gasoline on him, but he would stand frozen in her lap until they let him go.

His new home was an interesting-smelling place with a big human, probably male, who others called The Fireman, and who came in only in the early morning. Purple tried to get out so he could jump on things and maybe find another cat to chase. But the windows were closed with invisible stuff, glass.

It got greener and brighter outdoors. He found a place where he could watch out the window. One day he heard chirping. Purple leapt up on the ledge to see what was making that delicious music. Songbirds outside were dancing a seductive dance in the sky. He pawed the air, afraid he would find that glass stuff that often invisibly blocked windows. But there was nothing there. Air and nothing more.

He glanced down. He was high up, safe from dogs and cars and demented women with gasoline. And the birds zagged crazy zigs from branch to branch. And suddenly something glinted, rising swiftly, beautiful and alluring. He could reach it, he could almost—

But memory stopped him from leaping into flight. He remembered the itching between his shoulder blades. The wings were gone. He remembered the huge pruning shears, meant to shape heavenly junipers and topiaries. If he jumped, he would fall, as he had when he'd jumped off that windowsill in Cleveland, Tennessee.

He meowed one sad, loud meow. And he continued to watch the silver rising thing until it was too far away to see. Before, he had felt frustration and panic. But now, for the first time in his life, he felt true loss.

———

Trevin came in one afternoon with the kitten. Why wasn't it getting bigger? Was it some sort of dwarf? At least the purple color had faded to gray.

"Here, Auntie. I brought you a cute little kitten. The Fireman told me I could bring it in. Remember that kitten you were going to give me?"

Bambi tried to tell him "Oh yes, the kitten was for him, and by the way, this was the same goddamn kitten." But of course she couldn't say anything.

Trevin put the kitten in her lap. "Pet it. See, Auntie? It likes when you pet it."

Actually, the kitten had stopped purring the minute it was in Bambi's lap. It froze, terrified.

Trevin picked up Bambi's left hand—he knew that the right didn't work—and placed it atop the kitten. Bambi tried to resist, but the warmth and softness had a sort of allure. To please Trevin, she made tiny petting motions.

And felt something odd.

There were tiny, jagged stumps on the kitten's shoulders. With clumsy fingers, she parted the fur and saw scarred stubs of —what?

Trevin shrugged. "It's like he was crippled. Maybe he used to have wings. You ever hear of cats with wings?"

A cat that could fly. Only now, like her, it was grounded.

Right then, she understood that the kitten wanted its wings back, just as she wanted to walk, and speak.

Purple felt the scary hands on his back and he flinched, ready to spring away the minute she began to hurt him.

But she started petting him.

He thought about this. It felt good.

He decided to give her a chance. He settled his soft, hypnotic weight into her lap.

Bambi knew she was losing her mind. Trevin had gone home. The annoying girl in blue jeans who tried to make her stir pretend oatmeal vanished. Instead, impossibly tall men in white stood over her and scolded softly. "Your latest sun is sinking fast; your race is almost run," they said. "Your second chances now are past; your trial has begun."

Next afternoon she woke up with a screaming headache. She lay still on a gurney while they rolled her and drove her (In her own truck? Where was her truck? Had somebody remembered to renew her plates?) to another hospital.

Trevin came to see her in the other hospital. He talked about the cat some more. Said he'd nagged his mom until she finally looked in the garage, but there was no cat. No cage, either. "I wanted a kitty," he said. "Or maybe a puppy. Dogs are nice, too." He was making conversation. "Auntie, are you listening to me? I wish you could talk."

You and me both, kid.

One afternoon after Trevin had left, the white, tall guys came back. They put a long black cape on her and made her stand up and walk to the door. She looked back and saw herself slumped over her meal tray.

It was that gummy stuff. Even the water was gummy. She was glad she didn't have to eat it ever again.

The six guys in white took her to a huge warehouse, or maybe an airplane hangar, and put her in a new shiny wheelchair. The angels (now she knew they must be angels) stood over her. The one with slit pupils said, "You have learned nothing. My brethren assign you to the outer darkness. Please present your wrists and ankles for binding."

Bambi found she could move her legs and arms quite well.

She didn't want to be bound. Yet shame made her comply. One angel, the tall one who had processed her before, moved forward and tied a silver band around her wrists. He bent and began binding her ankles similarly.

"No, wait," she said, amazed that she could speak, despite the months of fruitless therapy. "I can't help that damn cat, and I can't love or forgive him for being a cat, but I feel sorry for him. He wants to fly, but you've grounded him. It was you, wasn't it?" She looked straight at the angel with slit pupils.

He gazed back with seraphic impassivity.

She spoke as clearly as she could. "He wants wings. You should give him his wings back." She had no idea how she knew this, but it was true.

The slit-pupiled angel spoke calmly. "That is impossible. He is a killer and his punishment was to lose the wings Heaven accidentally gave him."

Six angels seized her wheelchair like a queen's palanquin and lifted it, walking purposefully toward a dark door she hadn't noticed before. Beyond, she sensed wrenching cold darkness and smelled foul dead things. She cried out, "No, please!" But they marched her toward the dark opening, and when she was at its threshold she saw to her horror that it opened into a wide shaft, going on forever downward, like a drop tower she had once seen, in which lead shot was made.

And she was to be that molten shot, falling forever, until her soul congealed into a ball of lead.

"Make him mechanical wings, then!"

"Still, wings," said the slit-pupiled angel. But the six angels had paused.

"A rotor, like a helicopter, then," she said, and was surprised that she was weeping not for herself, but for something innocent and free that had been sentenced to fall forever. For anything innocent, even her younger self. For all children learning for the first time of death. For the purple kitten. "How can a dumbshit cat know right from wrong?"

"Helicopter," said the slit-pupiled angel thoughtfully.

And they set her wheelchair down gently at the very brink of hell's portal.

The big man didn't come home that morning. Purple knew he was The Fireman, and somebody had mentioned that firemen were often out late and sometimes had accidents. He liked the big man and hoped he would come home soon. Maybe he would take out the metal stick and make the little red dot race up and down the floor and walls. It wasn't as good as flying, but Purple liked it.

Purple woke to brightness and a breeze from an open window. The one called Bastael was standing in the air above the carpet in the bedroom. Purple blinked and stretched his claws.

Bastael touched Purple's fur, and Purple's back tingled and went numb. He no longer felt the ever-present ache of the phantom wings.

"This is a seed," said Bastael.

Purple felt a sharp pain, then a fullness, as if a warm hand pressed down on his back.

Bastael said, "You must leap from a short height. You will feel the axle extend from your back. It will grow to a height equal to your tail. Then the rotors will pop out from the top. They will begin to turn. Take care you don't catch your tail in them; they are soft and won't sever your tail, but it will be painful and may damage the rotors."

And the angel opened the window and scooped Purple up. In one motion, he threw Purple toward the ceiling.

And Purple felt the unfolding of a whip-strong stalk from between his shoulders, and from it like umbrella spokes, iridescent, translucent blades, and he purred and purred until they spun too fast for sight, whirring an answer to his purr, and he felt himself catch the air and, panicking, try to control his flight, and yes! yes! he was headed toward that window, and he would just make it, and he was through, out into the cold sunshine, and the ground was below, and it was further and further as he rose and slipped this way and that like a dragonfly, like a giddy child on a swing, darting and soaring, spying a bird, a blue jay that swooped toward him, then frantically changed its mind and batted its wings to get away, but he was in pursuit, flying, flying, flying faster, the Earth way below, the houses and trailer like little boxes—

And he was like no other creature that has ever been as he soared and darted and rejoiced in flight.

And Heaven forgot that his name was Joseph Patrick Michael Thomas Stephen Jesus-Marie Francis Antony Benedict Anselm John Edward, because he was no longer of Earth or of Heaven, he was only Purple, eternal creature of the air.

Trevin climbed into the passenger's seat of the Peterbilt cab.

"We have to sell it, honey," his mother called up to him, meaning the truck.

He placed his toy helicopter carefully on the driver's seat. "This is for Aunt Bambi."

"She's not coming back, Trevin. She's in Heaven."

He spun the helicopter rotors with his fingers. "Maybe."

THE HUNTER'S MOTHERS

My new mother gave me milk in a bowl,
groomed me with her large smooth paws,
held me, not in her mouth like my first mother,
but in her big lap, where I fell asleep.

I watched her each day, carefully,
so she could teach me to groom,
and hunt, and mate, and do whatever
was catly for me to perform.

She cut meat that she had caught
somewhere, and put it on plates as big as me
for her other kittens, the large bald ones.
But she never let me have the knife

nor let me play with the meat. Was I unworthy?
I went to the door, thinking she would take me
out in the grass and teach me to hunt.
But she said no.

And when I did go out, she stayed inside
and taught me nothing of hunting.
Perhaps I was too small, my claws too blunt
to catch meat for her and her unfurry kittens.

With practice, I caught a small meaty thing
that wriggled until I batted it to stillness.
Rather than eat it at once, I took it to Mother.
She screamed and threw it away.

Was it not large enough?
Was it not good meat?
I could not get it out of the big can where she puts
uninteresting vegetables and bones.

Later I caught others, but never one she liked much.
So I ate them myself, including
the ones that could fly, which I knew
Mother especially did not like.

I have lived a long time with Mother.
Her two-legged kittens grew up big, and ran away.
She grooms me when I sit on her lap,
but does not thank me for what I catch.

I know I am an unworthy hunter,
but how could I learn, when she never taught me?
Maybe she knew I was not as clever as the big meat
that she catches to put on the high table.

So I sleep in a patch of sun
and dream of my first mother,
who went away, but first taught me
I have claws.

PRIDE

THE HOT FUR thing under Kevin's shirt clawed at his chest. *Nice going*, he thought. *First the bum rap for weed, and now if I don't get caught stealing lab animals, I'll get rabies from this freak.*

Frankenlab, at Franken U, AKA Franklin Agricultural College, was messing with animals, electrodes in their brains, cloning them like Dolly the Sheep. Except not regular animals. Dead animals from frozen meat. And they were going to kill the animals.

He couldn't save them all. Those fuzzy, orange-furred mice, most wouldn't make it. Those guys from Animals Our Brethren had pried open cages, and when the mice wouldn't come out, they shook them out, and when the mice squeed, cowering under lab tables, they kicked them until they ran into corners, and from there may God have mercy on their itty souls.

Kevin petted the little monster through his shirt, but it writhed around and gummed him. "I'm saving your life, dumb-ox!" He dashed out of the building minutes before alarms brought the fire department.

Kevin had been in trouble before. A year ago, his girlfriend's cousin Ed and he had been cruising around in Ed's van, which had expired plates. Kevin didn't know about the baggie of pot under the driver's seat. When the state patrol started following, Ed asked Kevin to switch places. His license, like the plates, was expired, he said. They switched, veering madly, on a lonely stretch of 422. When they finally stopped and the cops asked to search the van, Kevin shrugged and said okay.

"And whose is this?"

Ed said, "Not me." Kevin was too surprised to look properly surprised, and this was a zero-tolerance state. So Ed got off with a warning, and Kevin, stuck with court-appointed counsel, served thirty days.

Kevin had been looking for a job to pay for college, when local papers broke the story that some thousand-odd animals (most, admittedly, mice) would be killed because their experiment was over. What was he thinking of? He wasn't an animal-rights kind of dude. Still, he felt panicked exultation fleeing the scene of the crime.

He struggled to control his Pinto while driving with the squirming thing scratching inside his shirt. He fumbled the back door key and pounded downstairs to the basement, where he pulled the light cord above the laundry tub and took the furball out of his shirt.

"Oh God, what have they done to you?" It was deformed: big head, chopped-off tail. Cat? Dog? A mix?

He deposited it in the laundry tub. Boggling at the size of its mouth, he realized it needed food. Now.

Forward pointing eyes. Meat-eater. Quiet, so as not to wake his mother, he ran upstairs and grabbed a raw chicken breast from the fridge. He held it out to the cub.

The cub flopped down on its belly in the tub, and tried to howl. All that came out was a squeak.

He tried to stuff the meat into its mouth, but it flinched away and lay looking at him, sides heaving.

Maybe the mother chewed the food up for it. Mother? Not

hardly. This thing didn't have a mother. It was fucking hatched in Frankenlab.

Raised in farm country, Kevin liked animals. He sometimes even petted Rosebud, the town pit bull, when Rosebud wasn't into tearing people's arms off. If his parents had been rich, he'd be pre-veterinary at Franken U. Or a cattle rancher, or a discoverer of rare snakes.

He went back upstairs and retrieved a knife, hacked tidbits off the chicken breast, and put them in the cub's mouth. The cub sucked on them, famished. It got to its feet and seized his finger with its front paws. Head held sideways, it chomped down on his finger. It did have a few teeth, it seemed.

He jerked away. "Stop it, you little monster!"

Kevin, it's a baby. Duh.

Where would he get a baby bottle?

He opened a can of condensed milk from the pantry, dipped a chicken chunk in it, and let the monster suck milk off the meat. Twenty minutes later it either got satisfied, or gave up. Its little belly looked marginally bigger, and the can was empty, mostly spilled on the laundry tub or his tee shirt.

It stretched and unsheathed claws way too big for a little guy the size of a raccoon.

Kevin thought, *It'll purr now.* Instead, it washed its face, running front paws over those deformed big jaws.

And then, just when Kevin decided it was almost cute, it reached out a claw and pricked his arm, not enough to hurt, just to say, "More?"

"You're beginning to tick me off," he said. The cub's gaze radiated adoration. It licked his hand, nearly rasping his skin off.

Its fur was golden retriever blonde, its eyes the color of river moss. Green-eyed blonde, like Sara. Dappled coat, like freckles on Sara's sweet shoulders. Sara Jones: they were almost a couple before his arrest; now she acted distant.

The monster leapt out of the tub and landed on the floor. It shook itself, surprised at the fall.

He lay down and stared at it, eye to eye. "You need a name."

He was furious that they'd planned to kill it. It was harmless. Uh, maybe not harmless. Planning to get big, judging from those paws, each the size of cheeseburgers. But innocent.

"What the hell have I got myself into?" he asked it.

Its grotesque little face shone with trust.

With the knife he'd used to cut the chicken, and thinking of Sara Jones, he tapped the little monster on each shoulder, and said, "I dub thee Sir Jonesy."

For a week, he kept Jonesy locked in the root cellar. His mom either didn't know, or pretended not to. Rosebud, Mr. Trumbull's pit bull, kept getting off his chain and sneaking over to paw at the basement door. There was an article in the paper about the lab fire, but the lab animals were hardly mentioned.

The scientists downplayed it all. The animals had been slated for "sacrifice," Dr. Betty Hartley said. Federal regulations required that animals be euthanized at the end of an experiment, she said, plus the money had run out. Cold. "Sacrifice": nice euphemism. Like "put to sleep." Like anything ever woke up from that sleep. Sacrifice? What, were they going to dance around an altar and beg God to protect them from weird-ass animal zombies?

Dr. Hartley said she was sad that the animals had all died in the fire, but accidents will happen.

So now he couldn't let anybody in on his secret. It would be insane to let the scientists find the cub again and kill it. But Jonesy (the cub was female, he discovered) whined and shivered in the root cellar, so he brought it upstairs.

His mother was not pleased.

"Look, Mom. I know it's humongous for a kitten, but that's all it is. Pet it?"

She refused to touch it. "I don't care what it is, I don't want it in my house."

"Listen, they'll kill it if I take it back. It's cute, see?" He held it to his chest to minimize her view of the monstrous head. The fur on its back was rough, not silky like a kitten's. But it was warm and happy to snuggle.

"Cute? Kevin, I'll show you cute. I know you stole it from Frankenlab. It'll probably get up in the night and suck our blood."

"Shit, Mom. It eats milk, not blood. You can't just kick it out on the street like a—like a broken TV."

"Kevin, get a job. And get that thing out of my house."

But Kevin's mother was too tired to put her foot down.

The cub's teeth started coming in. On a diet of ground meat that Kevin got from dumpster-diving, it had loads of energy. It used the energy stalking Kevin and shredding everything in Kevin's room.

The eye teeth erupted. And erupted. And erupted. Not domestic cat teeth. Long as the fishing knife the cops had taken away from him when he was caught with the pot.

He woke up one morning to find the monster sitting on his chest, hungry or affectionate, as if you could tell even with a tame cat.

"Man," said Kevin, peering closer, "your mom should have sued your orthodontist."

The cub did not laugh.

Not a vampire, but those sharp, sharp teeth—

And then his mind chewed through a bunch of information and farted out the truth. Rumors of ice age frozen flesh? Cloning? Bingo.

The damn thing, scrutinizing him with gold-green eyes, opening its huge mouth in a silent howl, was a saber-toothed tiger.

"Woo, dude. I thought you were trouble before."

It would need lots more meat.

At first he bought cheap cuts, then when he realized his

money from mowing lawns wasn't cutting it, he abstracted food from his own meals and from the refrigerator. And of course there was dumpster-diving. Restaurants, too.

One day, he found his mother in the kitchen, her hand bandaged. He hoped the bite was from Rosebud, but if Rosebud had bitten her, she'd probably be a mangled corpse.

He sank into a chair, while the sabertooth attacked the stinky mess he'd brought home for it.

"That's it, Kevin. You're my only son, the light of my life, a good, smart boy although way too trusting, but that cat is out by tonight or I call the cops." She blew her nose on a crumbled tissue. "I know where he came from."

Kevin didn't blame her. She was tired from overwork, just wanted to be left alone and sleep more than five hours at a time. They'd been moderately affluent before Kevin's dad left. But Dad had a really good lawyer. The measly child support had stopped when Kevin had turned eighteen. Dad still sent birthday cards with a two-dollar bill in each.

"If the boy wants a college education, a job will make him appreciate it more."

Jobs, yeah, well. Jobs for twenty-one-year-old guys who've done even a little time aren't easy to come by. Odd jobs, maybe shoveling walks in winter. Kevin wasn't a drinker, so he didn't have AA networking to fall back on.

Also, the damn cub was too mischievous to leave alone for long.

The week before the cat nipped Mom, he'd come home from helping a neighbor get her hay in and found the cub playing with a large rat. When the sabertooth saw him, she grabbed the rat in her mouth and tried to run away. Thank God it had been a rat and not those ratty-looking poodles the Parks owned.

So, Mom was right. The cat needed a home.

Sara. Their beginning romance had aborted, but he ran into to her sometimes at the feed store. She'd understood Kevin didn't know about the pot. But she always said, "It's not a good time," if he wanted to come over to the farm, or ask her out, not that he had much money for dates.

Guess she didn't want to be with a loser.

But, hell, he could rise again. Many great men, millionaires, politicians, had a shady past.

Sara didn't hate him.

He put the cub in an appliance carton (it whimpered, but complied), wrapped it with pink and ivory paper and gold ribbon, and lugged it to the Pinto. The cub thrashed around inside the box on his front seat, while he drove like a maniac to Sara's farm. Sara's parents hadn't really worked the family farm much since her granddad died, just kept geese and a big garden, and when they moved south to escape the winters, Sara kept the farm. Kevin used to help out, before he went to jail.

He lost his nerve and left the gyrating package on her paint-peeled porch.

The phone was ringing when he got back.

"Kevin, what is this? It nearly took my arm off."

He breathed slowly. He'd enrolled in an anger management class while in jail, not because he had problems with anger, but because the textbook looked interesting, and he found the breathing helped calm him. "Sara, it's a saber-toothed tiger."

"They're extinct."

"Yeah, yeah, yeah, so's the Bill of Rights. But this thing is a clone. From frozen meat."

"And this concerns me how?"

"It's, uh—"

"Look, Kevin, I remember the Maine coon kittens you gave me. I love those cats. But this is different, no? You must have stolen this thing from the college. And that's not all. It's going to grow up and be really aggressive. And, well, also—"

"Sorry. I'll come and get her back. Don't let her out, though. I'm not sure she knows how to defend herself."

When he got to the farm, Sara acted nervous, but she kissed him, and they sat on the couch and talked, about Ed, about jail. They didn't have sex, but he got his hopes up they could reconnect. Jonesy, meantime, tried to shred everything in her living room. She had put out a bowl of hamburger, otherwise the cub might have started shredding their clothes.

"It's not exactly cute," she said.

Jonesy's whiskers were almost as amazing as her teeth. Long and delicate. She stalked everything in the room, even shadows.

Kevin watched. The cub would hunker down and wriggle her backside, then dart forward and roll upside down. The hunker/wriggle part looked like any cat, but he'd never seen an animal do a half roll while attacking. Did that have anything to do with the sword-like canines?

"Kevin, you know I love animals."

Kevin said nothing. Their shoulders touched, and he put his hand on hers.

She left it there. "Okay. Until you get a place of your own. Don't come visiting without calling, though." She withdrew her hand.

Somebody was living with her. Of course.

The arrangement lasted three weeks.

When he drove over in answer to her phone call, Sara was crying. Jonesy had killed one of her geese, a real achievement, since even Rosebud was loath to fool with the geese. City folk underestimate the savagery of geese. But when Kevin opened the door, he boggled at how much the sabertooth had grown. Jonesy had to weigh as much Rosebud now.

Oops. What if Jonesy had attacked Sara?

"I let her run," she said. "You can't keep an animal like this cooped up. And it killed Emily Dickinson." Emily Dickinson was one of her geese. She named her geese after women poets.

"What have you been feeding her?" He felt shame that he

hadn't offered to pay for Jonesy's food. As if he could. He had a sudden panic over the welfare of the two Maine coon cats, but they were dozing on the sofa. The sofa was shredded, but the cats were fine.

"I feed her canned dog food, but she's always hungry. I haven't seen a raccoon in the neighborhood for two weeks. Kevin, I don't know where you can take her, but she can't stay here."

Was Jonesy grown enough to survive on her own, on garbage, raccoons, and people's geese? "How did she learn to eat the raccoons?"

"When I separated them, Emily kind of—split open, you know—and Jonesy stood over Emily, and then, as if she was sorry for the poor goose, she bent over and started licking her feathers, and she tasted the blood, and all of a sudden—"

Kevin had seen barn cats experience this epiphany. They discover their toy tastes good. Most learned from the mother cat, but get them hungry enough—

"She doesn't bother the geese anymore. They run away. But then there's the deer."

Kevin looked at his baby monster. "Jonesy couldn't take down a deer."

"Maybe not, but she sure knows how to chase them. And I worry about Mr. Trumbull's cows."

Kevin stood. "Thanks for taking care of her."

She took his hand, then moved closer. They gazed at each other. Could he kiss her?

She stepped back. "Take her somewhere. Hey, what about your dad's old trailer?"

The trailer featured scarcely more than a bed and a mini-dinette, abandoned on the lot near his mom's apartment. Roof leaked, plumbing wasn't connected. No trailer park would let him in with that wreck.

Nor with an "exotic animal." Even if he could pass Jonesy off as a rescued bobcat or lion cub.

"I'll call around." He had brought a collar and leash, and he snapped these on Jonesy. Jonesy had been on leash before and didn't like it, but she trusted Kevin enough not to fight.

Kevin was becoming an expert on smilodons. They weren't even from the same branch of the Felidae family as lions and tigers, but still might live in families. He must seem to Jonesy like her mother or the leader of her—what did they call lion families?—pride.

He smiled at Sara, eyes full of hope.

"Go!" she said, shoving him playfully. The sabertooth bared huge teeth at Sara until she smoothed its back fur. "You can come back. Bring Jonesy if you can control her. Just call first."

He led the sabertooth to his car. His mind roiled with possibility. *Ask her!* he thought. *She's got a new guy, or she doesn't. Ask!*

Too many secrets in Kevin's life: an animal he couldn't give up and couldn't keep, and a girl he wanted and whose life had become a mystery.

"Cat," he said. "We ain't neither of us got no pride."

Kevin's uncle owned some unworked farmland twenty miles out of town center. He got permission to park the trailer there, planning to haul water and use cartridges for gas heat. He bought a generator and parked the trailer well back from the road.

Odd jobs weren't enough. His mom's restaurant needed a dishwasher. Since the owner knew him—and about the jail time—there was no background check problem. Kevin bought a flip-phone that didn't require a credit card, and the modern man out of his time and ice age cat went there to live their hard life.

College plans receded into mist. Maybe someday Kevin could write a book about this. He bought a cheap digital camera and started a journal of Jonesy's growth and behavior.

The sabertooth soon learned to paw open the refrigerator. Kevin was forced to keep only vegetables in it. To supplement the dog food, he brought home a cut-up chicken or a chuck steak every night. The restaurant owner let him have these instead of dinner on the job. Jonesy tore into this meat, sometimes before Kevin could get the wrapper off. Sometimes the wrapper would get impaled on the four-inch-long canines, and she would run around trying to scrape it off. Kevin fell down laughing the first time that happened.

Kevin's own meals were either vegetarian or eaten at the restaurant.

He bought a used copy of *Born Free* at a yard sale. Jonesy wasn't any kind of modern cat, but it was a start. The librarian found him treatises on the smilodons of North America, though he wasn't even sure that's what Jonesy was. He had to play it cool when the librarian got nosy about his interest in cloning.

Jonesy shredded any book he brought home. To her, books, like everything else, were toys. So his reading was restricted to the library and their internet computers, and since he didn't like leaving the cat alone when she was awake, he kept all his research in his head.

He couldn't keep the sabertooth penned up, any more than Sara could. So, after a few weeks, he let her off the long line he'd tied to the trailer, and watched her lope the perimeter of the mowed area, where the demolished farmhouse had set. The line wouldn't hold her anyway, if she wanted to get away. She would chew through chain, though it might damage her beautiful teeth.

She stopped periodically to smell things, and her ears perked at the passage of a bird.

Then she saw the fox, and he thought he'd have to change her name to Turbo.

Did she eat the fox? No doubt she'd caught it. No bloody carcass in the trampled down area where the chase had ended. But for two days later, Jonesy looked quite pleased with herself.

The rest of that summer, the winter, and spring, the sabertooth grew sleek and menacing, muscles moving smoothly under short tawny fur. One of her magnificent eyeteeth loosened. When it fell out, she let Kevin feel inside her mouth, and underneath where it had been, he felt a new sharp point under the gum. Which grew and grew and grew. The other side did the same, and one morning he awoke to her heavy paws on his chest and opened his eyes to see her monstrous white glistening sabers new and sharp and creamy white, each as long as the knife they used in the restaurant kitchen to hack apart beef joints.

Her inscrutable face and hot, moist breath made his heart jump with terror. But she was his companion; he had held her under his shirt. He had fed her milk.

He reached up and stroked her ears, which alone of her fur retained kittenish silkiness. Then, with the greatest caution, he touched her saber fangs. Smooth, like ivory knives. This meant she was—*Smilodon fatalis*? *Smilodon neogaeus*? Or the other genus —*Megantereon*? He couldn't tell; he was no paleontologist.

He called Sara, to share this experience. She picked up after two rings, and hung up. But not even Sara's rejection could spoil that moment.

He was the first man ever to touch a living *Smilodon*'s teeth, and survive.

Sara would call now and then to ask about Jonesy, or tell him about a job opening. He could leave the sabertooth with her during the day, she said.

But when he called, employers always knew he was the kid who went to jail for drugs. Such is rural town gossip.

Jonesy and he walked the perimeter of the farm every night, out of sight of the road. He'd been four years out of high school. College seemed much further away now. He thought, *Some would say I have no life. A dumbass job. Had good grades, could have gone to college, married a beautiful woman who owned land. Lost all that because I trusted the wrong person, didn't fight the system hard enough. Could have done better. But I've touched the saber teeth of a*

Smilodon, and if no other gift is given me in this life, that might be enough.

If Jonesy missed anything, she never said so.

Then Jonesy came into heat.

As she came insinuating up to him, dragging her butt against the floor, trying to hump the ragged sofa arm, beseeching him to do something, anything, he just said, "Kitten, I'd write you a personals ad, but your kind don't subscribe to the *Country Cryer.*"

Neutering, but how the hell would he pass her off as anything but what she was? The vet would remember the incident at Frankenlab, and all would be up. Another jail sentence for Kevin. Worse for Jonesy: "sacrifice" at the hands of the scientists.

He tried penning her in the trailer while he slept in the Pinto, but she started chewing through the metal window frame. He let her out, and she howled to get inside with him.

Next night, his cell phone rang.

"Kevin, Keith, whatever your name is. People hear that howling, don't know what it is. But I do."

Kevin's heart lurched. Caller ID said: B. Hartley. The scientist. He said, "You plan to 'sacrifice' her now, Dr. Hartley?"

"No, you dolt. Do I have to spell it out for you? I incited your stupid Animals Our Brethren people to start that fire so she'd get away."

He took it in. "She's in heat. What should—"

"She'll either go out of heat, or she'll attack somebody. She may even decide you're the lucky tom. Give her back to me."

"Was there another sabertooth? A male?"

"Of course not, you idiot."

He snapped the cellphone shut and threw it against a wall.

Jonesy disappeared into the woods behind French Lick Creek.

A week later she slunk back. Kevin waited, but she was not knocked up. How could she be?

He was pretty sure Jonesy was keeping down the deer and raccoon population, but nobody mentioned missing any dogs. Cats, maybe.

When he needed to go to work, he had to lock her in the trailer, and she gnawed at the door and chewed the knob. Thank God she didn't have opposable thumbs; she was smarter than most dogs and cats. And some people.

But heaven, even Kevin and Jonesy's twisted heaven, can never last.

He had to run an errand. The feed store, which closed in the evening, was the cheapest place to get her dog food.

How she got out and trailed him wasn't that hard to reconstruct. He'd been careless. As he walked out of the store, he nearly tripped over her sunning herself on the front steps.

And across the square was Rosebud. Rosebud wasn't supposed to be out, either, but Mr. Trumbull was pretty lax too.

Rosebud hated cats. And Jonesy smelled like a big, unneutered cat. Rosebud killed cats. Smart cat owners in French Creek Township kept their pets indoors. As to farm cats, thank God Rosebud couldn't climb trees.

Rosebud was across the square, urinating on a post. He stopped abruptly and put his leg down, tiny ears perked, nose twitching. Then he charged.

Halfway across the square, he suddenly changed his mind. Uncertain, he froze, then turned tail.

Jonesy wasn't a long-distance runner, but she was fast on a sprint.

What Kevin saw next was that weird *Smilodon* leap. Jonesy charged and without stopping, rolled to her back, hugged Rosebud's neck, then sank her saber teeth into the dog's throat. The dog heaved into the air, Jonesy rolled over on top of him, and the two struggled. Rosebud had no offensive weapons but his jaws, and he'd never had to defend himself before, so his struggles turned to spasms and in seconds, he lay still.

Jonesy straddled the dog and raised her bloodied jaws in a terrifying roar. Everybody ran out of the feed store, the diner, and the gift shop.

Jonesy lowered her jaws and began to tear pieces out of the dog's belly.

Kevin fought vertigo and nausea. Somebody yelled, "Anybody catch that on video?"

He charged across the square, screaming at Jonesy. Three guys tried to stop him, yelling, "It'll kill you!" but he slid to a stop by the scene of carnage and yanked on Jonesy's collar.

"He's crazy!" somebody yelled.

Kevin realized he was crazy. Jonesy weighed maybe five hundred pounds by now. He'd read plenty of accounts of people mauled by previously docile big cats. Why did he assume Jonesy was different?

But he had to get the cat away, before somebody with a gun thought to use it.

A small, strong hand gripped his wrist.

Sara. Sara had the rifle her grandfather always carried in her truck. It had been a fixture in the truck for so long he'd forgotten about it. Nor did he wonder why she happened to be in town that day.

She gave him a serious look, then handed him the rifle. "It's under control," she yelled at the gathering crowd. "Back off before somebody gets hurt."

The dog was mangled meat. Jonesy had ripped open its throat and its belly and was standing over it, sides heaving with desire, jaws quivering with hunger and triumph.

The crowd all took a step back.

"Get her in the truck," Sara said. "You can still control her, can't you?"

Jonesy roared again, a softer roar.

Very deliberately—he believed that crap about animals being able to sense fear, but also knew he could fake courage pretty well—he took a handful of the fur at the back of Jonesy's neck and said in a low growl, "Into the truck, bad girl."

And it was over. Jonesy lowered her head and her stump of a tail and climbed into Sara's truck. Kevin slammed the door.

Which left Sara and Kevin standing outside.

Sara was shaking. She reached up and grabbed Kevin's ears and kissed him hard, tongue and all. Breaking loose, she said, "You're an idiot! But, God almighty, you've got guts!"

What now? Kevin couldn't leave Jonesy inside the truck. First, the sabertooth would demolish the inside. Second, it was a nice spring day, sunny, and heat would eventually build up and kill her.

But he could no longer predict the cat's behavior. Jonesy's blood was up; she might boil over.

"We have to get her out of here before the cops come," said Kevin. He shrugged, grabbed Sara's keys, and sprang into the truck.

Jonesy didn't kill him. The rest of his life, he would wonder why. Because he was dominant? Because she loved him? Do top predators know love?

He let Jonesy out of the truck outside his trailer. She lingered, licking his hand and making begging grunts, so he opened one of the dog food cans. She took it away from him and rasped the horse meat out, then lay down in the grass.

He went inside and wept.

Yes, somebody had videotaped it. Not the two animals running toward each other, not Jonesy's karate-like attack, but the dog underneath Jonesy, thrashing, then still, and Jonesy pulling out intestines. The video played several times, always zooming on the dead pit bull, then panning to Kevin pulling the cat away. He lay on the bed staring at the ceiling.

Thank God the cat looked like a female lion in the video. Some bystanders remarked on its teeth, but nobody connected it with the break-in and fire at the lab a couple years previous.

In the evening, Sara brought his car back. He didn't know how she'd started it, but she came in uninvited and lay beside him on the bed.

They kissed. She said, "Lock the door."

He did, obediently. "It won't stop Jonesy, if that's what you're thinking."

Hours later, they dressed and talked about hunting for Jonesy. Did anybody recognize them from the video? It was really jerky. Nobody was knocking on the door. But Kevin's mind roiled with possibilities: If somebody recognized Sara's truck, they'd go to her house, then figure she was here. They'd come with guns for Jonesy. Jonesy was tame; she wouldn't know to run.

Hellfire. Maybe Jonesy should be put down.

He said, "I always thought you still loved me a little. Unless this is just a stress reaction."

She leaned into him, then grabbed and shook him, hard enough that he thought, *She's going to slug me next.* She said, "I loved you, you jerk, but I couldn't keep on loving somebody who was stupid enough to go to jail for what he didn't do."

"Ed is your cousin. I couldn't rat out your cousin. And I never was sure the pot was his, anyway."

"Idiot!" And she did slap him, not enough to hurt, then turned away, hiding tears. "Ed is a goddamn jerk. He got you in trouble, you shielded him. He's my blood, but nobody I'd ever choose for family. Kevin, Kevin. I can't be with a man who spent time in jail and who—who lives with this monster."

"You like animals."

She sobered. "I do. I'm not sure what you should do with Jonesy. Maybe we could get rid of her somehow? Not kill her. Find somebody who would take her and keep her safe. Would you do that if I asked?"

"And we'd be like before?" He didn't say, "And you'll marry me," but he hoped she'd know that's what he meant.

"We'd at least solve a problem. I have a friend who knows how to sell things on the Internet. Remember those people who tried to sell their kid on eBay?"

"They got caught."

"They were stupid. eBay's not the option I had in mind. Listen, Ed isn't the only shady character we know. Maybe we can find a place for her."

He was reluctant. "Sara, don't get her killed."

He stayed up drinking cola after she left, but fell asleep in his lounge chair and awoke to early light and his cell phone ringtone.

"It's happened," said Hartley.

"What?" He thought she was talking about the attack on Rosebud.

"Sara Jones, that's your girl, right? The cat's over at her farm."

"Yeah, but Sara will be okay. Jonesy loves Sara."

"Judas Priest, boy, that cat is a top predator. Her definition of love is different from yours and mine. Big cats seem okay for years, then go off like a bomb and eviscerate somebody for no reason. For hunger. For a mate. Because a fly bit them on the nose."

"She loves Sara—"

"Yeah, she loves you, too. And maybe she thinks Sara is a rival in love."

That sounded crazy. But Kevin pulled his clothes back on and ran to his car.

He beat the police cruisers to the farm.

Jonesy was bashing the front door, roaring her earsplitting roar, not the roar of triumph she'd roared over Rosebud, not the roar of desire she'd yowled in heat. This was rage. And she was destroying the door.

As the first cruiser threw open its door and a cop sprang out with weapon drawn, the door imploded, and Jonesy bounded inside.

Why had he thought Sara was safe? For some reason—oh God, maybe it was sexual rivalry—Jonesy was after her.

Kevin bolted out of his car and up the porch stairs.

Inside, he smelled the fury of big, enraged cat.

"I'm up here!" Sara screamed.

He pounded up the stairs three at a time.

Sara's voice came from the upstairs bedroom. Outside that closed door, Jonesy reared on her back feet, head scraping the ceiling. She clawed at the doorknob, chewed at the door panels.

One door panel split and fell inward. Jonesy threw herself with renewed rage, and the door splintered.

"Here girl! Bad girl!" Why hadn't he thought of bringing meat?

No. Meat wouldn't work.

Sara was screaming, punching at the jammed window.

He raced up and grabbed the cat's collar, but she turned and knocked him flat.

As he lay gasping from the blow, Jonesy lunged for Sara.

He crawled, dizzy, trying to rise despite the agony in his chest. He just reached the door when Jonesy rolled across the floor, sprang up, and sank her teeth into Sara's throat.

Sara's eyes went wide, green as Jonesy's eyes. Her head snapped back. The cat ripped out her flesh together with a piece of her tee shirt, then howled, head thrown back, whiskered black nose grazing the ceiling light fixture.

Then the cat leapt through the window, splintering the frame.

Kevin crawled over to Sara. Her head was nearly separated from her body, blood gushing everywhere, in her beautiful golden hair, on her torn shirt, the cracked linoleum floor. More blood than he had ever seen.

He buried his face in the hollow between her breasts and sobbed.

Then he rose and looked out the window. Jonesy was loping into the barn.

He felt his way down the stairs, shattered. Sara was so beautiful. And Jonesy, his charge, his responsibility, his pet, had killed her. Pet? Oh, no. Not a pet. No more than an astronaut would call the moon a pet. No more than a composer would call his greatest symphony a pet. No more than a mountain climber would call Everest a pet.

He stumbled out into the light. Five police cruisers ringed the house now, and a paramedic van. One of the paramedics had the rifle from Sara's truck.

"Cat still in there?" one cop yelled.

"Sara's upstairs. She's dead," Kevin said. He sank to his knees and sobbed.

Hartley appeared. "The cat ran into the barn. I saw it."

The paramedic raised the rifle, and another cop hauled open the barn door. He had a German Shepherd with him on a short leash. Kevin pulled himself erect.

The dog strained forward, then turned to cower behind the cop. The cop broke into a run, at the same time trying to unholster his service revolver.

Jonesy exploded out of the barn. The cop with the dog fell down and Jonesy vaulted over them.

Kevin heard the sound of the rifle being cocked.

Kevin screamed, "No!" He launched himself at the rifleman.

The rifleman stumbled and the shot went wild.

A tawny streak—Jonesy—broke into the woods behind the barn and coursed out of sight.

Hartley screamed, "Why did you do that?"

"Killing the cat won't make Sara be alive again."

"You're in denial! The *Smilodon* will kill again."

Kevin was silent. Hartley was right. He had no idea why he

had pushed the rifleman. He felt his arms being jerked back, cuffs cut his wrists. But the sabertooth, the miracle from another world, was free.

"You were involved with Sara Jones," Hartley said. "I thought you loved her."

"I did. Not what matters."

"This monster kills the woman you love, and you protect it?"

How could he explain?

———

Jonesy was never found, though attacks on domestic animals and deer increased in the county for a few weeks. Maybe the sabertooth died, maybe she went north, where the woods were thicker and the game larger.

Kevin went to jail. He got most of a college degree in there, gratis the state. He wasn't street smart, that was obvious, but he had a talent for book learning.

His life had changed forever. He got out of jail, went to university, studied paleontology, but studiously avoided Franklin U and Dr. B. Hartley, though she begged him for his photos of the *Smilodon*.

He never married.

But he had companioned a *Smilodon*, brought back from the deeps of time. It had been like stepping on the moon. He had touched its white, saber-like teeth. And it made him immortal.

It was enough.

ADDITIONAL COPYRIGHT INFORMATION

ABOUT THE AUTHOR

Mary Turzillo loves cats and story-telling. Her "Mars Is No Place for Children" won a 1999 Nebula, and her *Lovers & Killers* won the 2013 Elgin Award. *Sweet Poison*, with Marge Simon, was a Stoker finalist and Elgin winner. Mary has been a British SF Association, Pushcart, Stoker, Dwarf Stars, and Rhysling finalist. Her recent books are *Mars Girls* (Apex, 2017) and *Bonsai Babies* (Omnium Gatherum, 2016).  She fenced foil for the US at Veteran World Championships in Germany, 2016. She lives in Ohio, with scientist-poet-fencer Geoffrey Landis, plus Scaramouche, Samurai, Azrael, and Tyrael, the last four of whom appear to be cats.

OTHER WORDFIRE PRESS TITLES

Taylor's Ark
by Jody Lynn Nye

A Furnace Sealed
by Keith DeCandido

Madrenga
by Alan Dean Foster

Our list of other WordFire Press authors and titles is always growing. To find out more and to shop our selection of titles, visit us at:
wordfirepress.com

facebook.com/WordfireIncWordfirePress
twitter.com/WordFirePress
instagram.com/WordFirePress
bookbub.com/profile/4109784512

CPSIA information can be obtained
at www.ICGtesting.com
Printed in the USA
LVHW101202141022
730646LV00002B/309